DAWN LEE MCKENNA'S

RIPTIDE

A *FORGOTTEN COAST* SUSPENSE NOVEL: BOOK TWO

2015

A SWEET TEA PRESS PUBLICATION

First published in the United States by Sweet Tea Press

Edited by Tammi Labrecque
larksandkatydids.com

Cover by Shayne Rutherford
darkmoongraphics.com

Interior Design by Colleen Sheehan
wdrbookdesign.com

For Uncle Jim

Thank you for believing in me

CHAPTER
ONE

The sky over Apalachicola Bay, in the Florida panhandle, had just gone from orange to pink, and then blue. Here and there, small, wooden oyster skiffs dotted the shallow waters, punctuating the start of the long oystering day.

Further out, larger shrimp boats, their nets spreading like pterodactyl wings, were coming to the end of their day. One of those boats belonged to Axel Blackwell, whose twenty-seventh cigarette was dangling from his lips as he watched his crewmen, Daryl and Petey, swing the second shrimp net over to hover above the deck.

Axel was tired and irritated. They'd been out since seven the night before, trying to harvest enough shrimp to pay the two crewmen, pay Axel, and still have money to pay for the fuel they'd need tomorrow night.

Shrimping was all Axel did and all he'd ever wanted to do. His father had made his living with this same boat for forty-five years, and his father's father had died doing it, due to an unfortunate mixture of fuel leak and chain smoking.

Axel had come out to the bay straight from high school, and he was going to eke a living from it until either they drained the Gulf or the oil companies did it in for good.

He weighed the net with his eyes as Daryl moved in to untie the rope at the bottom that held it shut. This was a good load. As long as there were some nice big ones in there among all the peewees, they'd do all right.

Daryl, big as a truck and blacker than good dirt, yanked the knot loose and stepped back as the load poured out in a rush, spreading out somewhat before piling up in a heap at the center. Petey, small, wiry, and gray in the beard, hopped over a writhing sea trout as it slid right at him.

They all stared at the three hundred or so pounds of sea life and seaweed.

"Oh, my sweet dear Jesus," Daryl said quietly.

Petey leaned over the side and threw up into the bay.

The tip of Axel's cigarette flared up as he inhaled, then he let a finger of smoke escape his clenched lips.

"Crap," he said. "We might want to get that crab off that foot there."

⚓   ⚓   ⚓

Maggie Redmond's long, dark hair whipped around her face as she ran the Sheriff department's speedboat at full throttle across the bay. She turned around and looked at Wyatt Hamilton, her boss and the Sheriff of Franklin County, who was standing just behind her, holding onto the starboard rail.

"Hey!" she called. He looked over at her. "Steer for a second, would you?"

Wyatt stepped over and took the wheel, and Maggie dug a ponytail holder out of her jeans pocket and restrained her hair. She was short to begin with, but standing next to Wyatt, who was six-feet four, she always felt like she needed to stand up just a little straighter and display her holster a little more prominently.

Maggie took the wheel again, and Wyatt remained standing next to her.

"You know Axel Blackwell?" he yelled over the engine.

"Yeah, we went to high school together," she yelled back.

"Straight shooter?"

Maggie couldn't help laughing just a bit. "Yeah, you could say that."

They were silent for a few minutes, as they passed St. George Island to the left, which sat five miles or so off the mainland. Hwy 300, or the causeway, or the bridge, depending on who was talking, connected St. George Island to the mainland like a suspended shoestring.

Maggie turned away from the sight of the bridge and focused on the water. Last week, a damaged but courageous young girl had floated off of the bridge in her pale yellow dress, having decided that dying was better than living the only life she'd been allowed to live.

After a few minutes, Maggie pointed out to the west.

"There's it is," she yelled.

It took them just a few more minutes to reach Axel's boat, the *Ocean's Bounty*, which had dropped anchor before Axel called Maggie.

Axel leaned over the port side as Maggie cut the engine and coasted over, then he grabbed the line Wyatt tossed at him. Maggie dropped a couple of bright orange bumpers into the water to keep the boats from scraping each other.

Maggie reached over to the bench seat and picked up her red crime scene case, a tool box really, and stepped up on the bench.

Wyatt stood aside and let Axel hand Maggie aboard first, then he grabbed Axel's hand and did the same. Maggie and Wyatt both stopped in the middle of the deck and looked at the pile in front of them. Wyatt sighed, then looked at Maggie and waggled his eyebrows.

"Hey, Maggie." Axel leaned back against the helm, drinking from an aluminum travel mug. "How's it going?"

Maggie looked over at him and smiled. Axel had always been her favorite among her ex-husband David's friends. They'd grown up together, and if she hadn't loved David since fifth grade, she probably would have gone for Axel, though that would have been a mistake. He was a looker, in that rough, slightly scruffy way that some men were, but he wasn't exactly marriage material, as his two former wives would attest.

"Not much, Axel, what's going on with you?" she asked, setting her case down beside her.

His green eyes squinted under his beanie as he grinned. He pointed at the pile of shrimp with his hand. "We got an extra foot in our last load."

Wyatt and Maggie, both with their hands on their hips, stared down at the pile of several hundred shrimp and one human foot that laid on the deck.

"Well then," Wyatt said after a minute.

Maggie looked at Axel. "Where are the guys?"

"Below," he said, taking off his beanie and running a hand through his brown hair before slapping the hat back on. "Daryl's still discussing the situation with Jesus, and I got tired of watching Petey throw up his shredded wheat."

Maggie nodded as she looked at the foot. It was actually most of a calf as well as a foot. Most of the flesh from the calf had been nibbled away by the sea life, leaving just the tibia and fibula bones to represent a former leg. The foot itself, however, was mostly intact. In fact, it still wore a man's Docksider and a brown sock, which, without any flesh to hang onto, had crumpled around the bottom of the ankle. According to the shoe, they had a right foot on their hands.

"Did you guys touch it or anything?" Wyatt asked.

"Well, I tried to roll his sock up for him, but it didn't take."

"You're such a jerk," Maggie said, trying not to smile.

Axel nodded in agreement as he lit another cigarette. "Yeah, but my kids seem to like me."

Maggie pulled a pair of blue latex gloves out of her case and started snapping them on. "Is this all that's here? I mean, did you sift through the rest?"

"We kicked it around a little. There's nothing else in there that's not supposed to be."

Maggie reached over and lifted the leg up a little by the end of the fibula. "Well, he wasn't eaten by a shark," she said, lifting the foot a little higher as Wyatt leaned over to look.

"It's been cut," he said.

Maggie turned the foot to get a look from the other side. "Yeah."

Axel whistled around his cigarette. "You sure it's a guy?"

"Yeah, look at the shoe." Maggie turned the leg upside down to look at the sole. "Size 10."

"I haven't seen any missing persons reports come in lately, have you?" Wyatt asked.

Maggie broke her neck looking up at him. "Uh-uh."

"If his DNA's not in CODIS, we might have a little trouble identifying this guy," Wyatt added.

"Yeah," Maggie laid the foot back down.

"If it was me, I'd start lookin' around town for somebody with a peg leg," Axel offered.

Maggie and Wyatt both shot him a look, then Maggie stood up and pulled off her gloves.

"Well, Larry will be here in a few minutes to have a look," she said, referring to the elderly medical examiner. "Dwight's bringing him out."

She looked back toward St. George Island and saw a speedboat off near the tip. "There they are."

She pulled her digital camera out of her case, dropped her gloves on the deck, and handed the camera to Wyatt. "Here, you take better pictures than I do."

"That's because I have an artistic eye," he said.

He squatted down and started taking shots of the foot, while Maggie walked over to Axel.

"Give me a sip of that coffee. You woke me up."

Axel smiled and handed her the travel mug. She turned it up and took a drink, then choked a bit before swallowing.

"Bourbon, Axel?"

"Hey, this is my happy hour, Maggie. Except I'm not especially happy."

Maggie nodded and looked at the pile of shrimp. "I'm sorry, Axel. You know you're gonna have to throw them all back."

"I don't know why," he answered. "This is my golden hole, Maggie. You know I'll probably catch half of 'em again tomorrow night."

"Yeah, I know. But we won't know that for sure."

"I'll be honest with you, I was within a gnat's ass of throwing that thing back over the side. This is a pretty nice haul."

Maggie nodded again as she watched Wyatt get some pictures from the other side of the foot.

"I know. I don't blame you," she said.

A few minutes later, Wyatt helped Larry Wainwright, white-haired and crane-like, board the *Ocean Bounty,* as Deputy Dwight Shultz held his black leather case for him.

"Well, well," Larry said, as he peered at the foot over his bifocals. He grabbed Wyatt's hand to hold himself steady as he gingerly knelt down.

They watched him lean in and stare at it up close for a minute.

"What do you think, Larry?" Wyatt asked.

Larry looked over his shoulder and craned his neck to look up at Wyatt. "Well, it's not a good candidate for reattachment, I can tell you that."

CHAPTER

TWO

A fter taking the statements of Axel and his crew, Maggie and Wyatt took the department boat back to the dock the SO used in Apalachicola, just next to Sea-Fair, Bennett Boudreaux's seafood processing business.

The Franklin County Sheriff's Office was located in Eastpoint, connected to Apalachicola on one side by the John Gorrie Memorial Bridge and to St. George Island on the other by Hwy 300 or the causeway.

Apalachicola was a throwback to an earlier time, and looked more like coastal Connecticut than most people's visions of Florida. Located in the Panhandle, about an hour southwest of Tallahassee, it was primarily a fishing town, famous for its Apalachicola oysters and Gulf shrimp. Like nearby Gulf towns in Alabama, Mississippi and Louisiana, Apalach had been hit hard by disasters both natural and oil-made, but it had a small tourist trade that managed to keep it afloat when fishing and oystering got hard.

Tourists came for the oysters, the fishing, the beaches of St. George Island, and the nine hundred historic buildings turned into gift shops, nautical art galleries, and restaurants. The town had one traffic light, a passing acquaintance with severe weather, and fewer than three thousand residents. It had been Maggie's home her entire life and she loved it, and the people in it, fiercely.

After getting the boat stowed away, Maggie and Wyatt walked across the oyster shell parking lot toward their cars. Maggie was just under five-foot three, and with her slight frame and long, dark brown hair, she looked younger than her thirty-seven years, especially walking next to Wyatt. Wyatt was eleven years her senior and stood more than a foot taller. His moustache was also quite a bit more impressive than Maggie's, and the tinge of gray in his thick brown hair lent him an air of dignity that his dimples and occasional goofiness tended to ruin. But, while he had a knack for one-liners and a laid-back demeanor, he was sharp, dedicated, and occasionally intimidating.

He and Maggie approached their cars, his department cruiser and her ten-year old black Jeep Cherokee, and Wyatt took off his SO cap, and ran a hand through his damp hair before putting the hat back on.

"So what do you think?" he asked.

"You got me," Maggie answered. "It looked a little too neat for a propeller."

"Yeah. I didn't see anything that looked like a nick on the rest of the leg bone there."

"I don't know," Maggie said. "Drug deal gone bad?"

"Maybe." Wyatt leaned up against his door. "So, I've been thinking about our first date."

"Yeah? Did we have fun?" Maggie asked, smiling.

"You're precious. No, I was thinking that we should have one."

Last week, after several months of occasional light flirtation punctuated by the odd mutual stare, Maggie and

Wyatt had had what Wyatt now called "The Test Kiss". The test, on Wyatt's part, was whether Maggie was genuinely interested in him. On Maggie's part, it was an experiment to see if she could be comfortable kissing anyone other than the ex-husband that she had loved and been best friends with since fifth grade.

They both passed, but a Sheriff dating one of his two investigative officers would not go over very well, although if he were dating Terry Coyle, it would be even less well-received, especially by Terry's wife.

"Well, I'm okay with that," Maggie said. She opened her cargo door and put her crime scene case inside.

"Good. I was thinking you should come to my house for dinner."

"You want me to come to your house for our first date?"

"Well, it is more fun if we're both in attendance."

"Isn't that a little more questionable than being seen out in public?"

"People see us eating out together all the time," Wyatt said.

"Yeah, with guns on, in broad daylight."

"The Jorgensen's are in bed by seven and the guy that lives on the other side of me has an illegal cable hookup, so I don't think he's going to be a problem."

Maggie smiled at him. "Do you cook?"

"I am a man, as an investigator of your caliber has probably noted. I grill."

"David cooked on the stove, too."

"David is a pantywaist," Wyatt said mildly. "Do you want to come?"

"Yeah, of course I do."

"Then that's what we'll do. Tomorrow night okay?"

"Okay."

"Okay." He stared at Maggie, as though he wasn't sure what to say next.

"Do you need me to sign something?" she asked, grinning.

"Or we could skip it."

"I'm kidding. Yeesh."

Wyatt grinned at her and pulled his keys out of his pocket, opened his door.

Maggie opened her own door. "Hey, we still have some time before Woody goes to press," she said, speaking of the editor of the town's weekly paper. "I think we should give this to him, see if he'll find room for it."

"Well, he'd probably have to ruffle some feathers over at the Junior League, boot the coverage of their bi-monthly meeting."

"Maybe some oysterman or shrimper saw something out on the Bay that he doesn't know he saw yet."

Wyatt nodded. "Maybe. Why don't you run over there and ask him?"

"I can't. He's still pissed at me."

"Oh, yeah," Wyatt said.

In last week's edition, he'd referred to Grace Carpenter, the young girl who'd jumped from the bridge, as 'a drug dealer's teenaged girlfriend'. She'd been much more than that, and Maggie had confronted him more loudly than she'd intended at Delores's Sweet Shoppe. It had ruined his appreciation of his morning cinnamon roll, and he hadn't spoken to her last Saturday when they'd seen each other at Battery Park.

"Never mind, I'll go," Wyatt said. "Why don't you go back to the office and see if we missed a missing person."

"Okay. I'll see you later."

They both got into their cars, and Wyatt let Maggie pull out first. She stopped halfway out and rolled down her passenger window.

"Maybe you should take him some cinnamon rolls," she said.

Wyatt put his car in gear and rolled his eyes at her. "Don't tell me how to do sheriff-y stuff."

⚓ ⚓ ⚓

Maggie was stopped at the one red light downtown, on Hwy 98, when she decided to make a right, rather than a left.

Apalachicola wasn't like other places on either of Florida's coasts. It didn't have any suburbs or McDonalds or even a Walmart, something of which the residents were quite proud. There was no sprawl; there was just downtown and not downtown. What Apalach lacked in square miles, it made up for with historic ambience. What it lacked in big commerce, it made up for with an actual soda shop and more than its fair share of good raw bars, in a per capita sort of way.

It was only a few blocks from the traffic light to the Apalachicola City Cemetery.

Maggie drove in, parked her Jeep, and walked between the graves and the palms and the live oaks. The sun was already blistering and its light was so harsh and so white that it faded what color there was in the old cemetery. Green became gray, gray became white and white just disappeared.

Although rare for the end of June, there was no rain in the forecast other than the usual summer shower, which arrived somewhere around three in the afternoon every day and evaporated by three-thirty. Maggie sucked a hot lung-ful of the morning air and wished for a tropical depression.

Maggie looked at the small, simple headstone, which said only *Grace Carpenter*, and below that *1996-2015*. Maggie and her parents had paid for the headstone, and Maggie had wanted it to say something more. Maybe to say that she was a good mother. But Grace had had her new-born taken away, as well as the two little children belonging to her now dead boyfriend, meth dealer Richard Alessi, because she'd been foolish and lonely and plain enough to fall in with a man like Ricky.

It hadn't mattered that Grace, bony and small and brave, had, of her own volition, put herself in danger by trying to help Maggie to arrest Alessi. It hadn't mattered that she'd done it to give her child, and his children, a bet-ter life.

Grace had known she wouldn't get her kids back, even though Maggie had promised to find help. Grace had known the workings of Children's Services better than Maggie did, and she'd driven to the bridge. It just didn't seem right to Maggie to mention on the headstone that she'd loved her children.

But the guys from the Sheriff's office and the Apalachic-ola PD had known, and they'd all chipped in to pay for the plot. It had been a small service, just Maggie and Wyatt and a few of the officers who had worked the Alessi case. Maggie had gotten her ex-husband, David, to come, and they'd stood under a tin-colored sky while he played *Way-faring Stranger* on his guitar. Then they'd all walked away and left her as alone as she'd been most of her short life.

Oddly, the casket had been paid for by Bennett Bou-dreaux.

Boudreaux was Apalachicola's version of a crime boss or head of a Mafia family, though he'd never been convicted of a crime and was Cajun by birth rather than Italian. He owned several seafood-related businesses in town and several in his home state of Louisiana. He sponsored community events, had his picture taken with local politicians, and his son Patrick was the Assistant State's Attorney for Franklin County. It was all very cozy and polite, but a lot of people were afraid of Boudreaux and most of them had a reason to be.

But Boudreaux had actually tried to use his influence to help Grace, at Maggie's request. It just hadn't come through in time.

Maggie squinted up at the sun and sighed. Then she kissed a finger, touched it to the headstone, and turned and walked away.

⚓ ⚓ ⚓

Wyatt walked into the old brick warehouse downtown that now housed Apalach's weekly newspaper, *The Apalachicola Press*, and smiled back at Maureen Dailey, the elderly lady who had been the receptionist/secretary/everything at the paper since the headlines had been about Vietnam.

"Why, how are you, Sheriff Hamilton?" she said over her computer monitor.

Wyatt walked up to her desk and took off his sunglasses. "I'm fine, Mrs. Dailey, how are you?"

"Fair to middlin'," she answered. "It's press day, you know. Busy, busy."

"Is Woody in?"

"Oh, no." She shook her head. "Well, that is, he's in, but no, don't talk to him today."

"Well, I have to, sorry."

"Can it not wait until tomorrow?"

"No, I need him to put something in the paper for me."

"Oh, no, that won't do." Mrs. Daily started fiddling with the chain on her bifocals. "The paper's almost set to go."

"It'll be all right, Mrs. Daily." Wyatt started heading toward the hallway that led to the press room and Woody's office.

"Oh, it won't," she said. "Mercy, I'll have to listen to him all day."

Wyatt walked back to the small office belonging to Woody Dumont, the paper's editor. The office was the only enclosed area in the back of the building. Beyond it was an open area with several desks, where reporters and other employees tapped away on their keyboards or squinted at ads and graphics on their monitors. Beyond the staff area was the actual press.

Woody, a slightly-built, balding, and chronically agitated man in his early fifties, was standing at a table against a windowed wall, inspecting a physical mock-up of the paper, with various articles cut and taped onto newsprint. Wyatt rapped on the door jamb and Woody looked over his shoulder.

"Oh, hey, Sheriff," he said cheerfully.

"Hey, Woody. I need you to do something for me," Wyatt said, walking into the office.

Woody turned around and craned his neck to look at Wyatt. "What do you need?"

"I need to you to put something in the paper for me."

"Tomorrow's paper?" Woody asked.

"Yes, please."

"Nope." Woody started shaking his head emphatically. "No, can't do that. I'm sorry."

"I need you to do it anyway," Wyatt said, trying to soften it with a smile.

"I can't," Woody said, waving a hand at the mock-up behind him. "Paper's all set."

"It can't wait for next week, Woody, and the *Press* could be instrumental in helping us solve a case."

"What case?"

"A shrimper found a foot in his net this morning. We're hoping maybe someone saw something that can help."

"A foot? What kind of foot?"

Wyatt looked down at his sizable shoes. "Just like the ones you and I still have."

"A human foot?"

"Yes. And we need to find out who it belongs to and whether anyone saw anything recently that might be important."

"Oh, this is awful! This is—oh, for crying out loud! A shark? Was it one of those ridiculous Bull sharks you think? It's those people shore fishing, you know."

"No, it wasn't a shark. This foot was cut. Chopped off."

Woody stared at Wyatt for a moment. "You mean deliberately?"

"That's the assumption, yes," Wyatt said patiently.

"Oh, well, dandy! That's even better. Half the people who read it will think we have sharks and the other half will think we have serial killers." Woody patted at his chest with his hands as though he were checking for something in his pocket, although he didn't have one. "This is not good for the tourists, Sheriff."

"Well, I realize that, Woody, but—"

"I mean, we're online and everything, now! The people out on St. George are gonna pack up and the ones getting ready to book their vacation rentals, why, they'll go to Destin or, heaven help us, Daytona, if they think we have sharks or serial killers."

"We don't have sharks and serial killers, Woody. Everybody knows serial killers don't hang out in Apalach."

"It could be a passing-through serial killer."

"Well, then he's gone," Wyatt countered.

"Where's the rest of the body?"

"Hell if I know."

"Oh, this is not good." Woody shook his head. "The rest of it's gonna wash up on the island and everybody's gonna be running up and down the beach with their arms in the air. It's gonna be like Amity Island all over again."

"That's not gonna happen, Woody."

"How do *you* know?"

"Well, in all likelihood, pieces would wash up on the beach, not a body missing one foot."

Woody gave Wyatt a stricken look and Wyatt held up a hand.

"I'm kidding, Woody." He pulled a piece of note paper out of his shirt pocket and held it out to the other man. "I wrote some notes down for you. Just keep it short and simple. I appreciate it."

Woody stared at the paper for a moment, as if not taking the paper might make the foot go away.

"Woody," Wyatt said firmly.

Woody reached out and took the note with two fingers. He shook his head slowly. "Between BP and storms and the feet, we just can't get a break down here."

Wyatt headed for the door. "Cheer up, Woody. The weather's looking good."

He waved goodbye to Mrs. Dailey, as he hotfooted it to the door before she could tell him how upset she was with him. The mid-morning heat blasted him as he stepped outside to the sidewalk. The air was humid enough to make him feel like he was wading to his cruiser rather than walking.

His door handle was scorching and he put a finger in his mouth to soothe it, then flipped at the handle a few times in an effort to open the door without actually touching it again. Once he got it open, he stood there with the door open to let the interior cool off a minute.

He looked down the street, lined on either side with cafes, gift shops, seafood restaurants and local art galleries. He didn't blame Woody for being upset. Apalach needed the tourists that flocked to it every summer.

Hopefully, most of the tourists would assume it was a gruesome murder, and God knew, they probably came from places where that kind of stuff happened all the time. But some people probably would assume it was a shark, and that probably would be bad for business. He sighed and slid into the car as he had a vision of Richard Dreyfus following him around Piggly-Wiggly, gesturing spasmodically and telling him he needed a bigger boat.

Maggie had spent two hours looking through missing persons and accident reports to no avail, when Deputy Myles Godfrey stepped into the doorway of the office she and Terry Coyle shared on alternating days.

"Hey, Maggie," Myles said.

"Hey, Miles," she answered, glad for the interruption.

"I just got back from running that parole violation over to Liberty County," he said, his eyes bright behind black-framed glasses. Myles always made her think of some young news anchor from the sixties. "What's this I hear about somebody finding a foot in a shrimp net?"

"Yeah. Axel Blackwell was the one that found it."

"Well, he would be, wouldn't he? Guy's got the weirdest luck." Myles licked his lower lip and shook his head. "This isn't going to be good for business."

"Well, we can't put it back."

"Yeah, I gotcha, but man."

Maggie felt for Myles. His wife was expecting their fourth baby and her gift shop was a good third of their income.

"Sorry, Myles."

"So it was cut?"

"Looks that way," Maggie answered. "Larry's working on it."

Maggie looked back at her monitor, and Larry knit his brows and stared into the air for a second. "Where do you suppose the rest of him is?"

"Pensacola, hopefully," Maggie answered.

"That would be nice."

Wyatt appeared in the doorway behind Myles, taking off his cap and wiping at his forehead with his arm. In his other hand, he held a gigantic bottle of Mountain Dew.

"Hey, Myles," he said.

"Hey boss, how are ya?"

"Evaporating."

"Yeah, man. July's a day early, huh?" Myles headed for the door, and Wyatt stepped in and aside to let him out.

"See ya, Maggie," Myles said, waving. Maggie smiled back and Myles headed down the hallway.

Maggie watched Wyatt head for the metal folding chair in front of her desk.

"Okay, so I've been all over marine accident reports and missing persons reports and there's just nothing."

Wyatt sat and stretched his impossibly long legs out in front of him. "Nothing?"

Maggie shook her head. "I've just started spreading the search a little, but nothing in Franklin, Gulf or even Wakulla Counties."

"Okay, so no one is missing this guy, at least, not yet." Wyatt took a long pull on his Mountain Dew. "We don't have even an approximate time of death yet, though Larry said—what—max ten days, right?"

"Yeah."

"So it's early yet. Maybe nobody knows he's missing."

"Maybe. I've just started to look in Bay County, but I'm waiting on Jeff to get me the data on tides and currents for the last ten days or so. Maybe we can get some idea of where he went in."

"Long shot until we have an idea of *when* he went in."

"Yes."

"Larry's DNA samples are on the way to Tallahassee. I called a friend of mine over there and called in a favor. He's going to try to get us in on a rush, so we may have something with CODIS sooner rather than later."

"That would be miraculous."

"It would." Wyatt screwed the cap back on his soda. "Meanwhile, I have a parole hearing." He stood up and stretched, and Maggie made a point of not noticing how attractive that was. "What's your next step?"

"I'm going to finish up with Bay County, then wait on Jeff before I waste any more time here," Maggie said. "Then I think I'll run over to Scipio Creek Marina and see if I can catch any oystermen coming in or shrimpers going out that may have seen something. Is Woody putting it in tomorrow's paper?"

"Oh, yeah. He's in an advanced state of agitation about it, but it's going in."

"Good. Another long shot."

"Yeah. They suck." Wyatt took his hat off, ran a hand through his wavy brown hair and plopped the cap back on his head. He gave her a wink as he headed out the door. "See ya."

"See ya," she answered, and watched him walk out into the hall. Then she went back to her screen.

⚓ ⚓ ⚓

A few hours later, Maggie parked her Jeep in the oyster shell parking lot at Scipio Creek Marina, used by pleasure boaters, shrimpers and oystermen alike.

Maggie got out of the Jeep, swam up through the humidity, and surfaced gasping for air. June had been typically stormy until the last week or so, and she longed for one of the coastal Panhandle's tremendous downfalls. One look at the almost white sky told her she didn't have one coming. It was almost four in the afternoon and there wasn't a breeze to be had.

She saw Mel Roland hosing down his oyster skiff, and walked down the dock to meet him.

"Hey, Mel," she called.

Mel looked up at her, a ring of pure white hair surrounding his skull, which was capped by a bald scalp riddled with sunburn scars, sun spots and probably a few precursors to melanoma.

"Hey there, Maggie!"

"You doing all right, Mel?"

"Right as I can be," he said." He turned off the hose, picked up a deck brush, and started scrubbing."

"Hey, Mel. You didn't happen to see anything odd out on the bay lately, or maybe a boat you didn't know?"

Mel stopped scrubbing and leaned on the handle, scratching at his cheek. "How lately?"

"Last week or so?"

"Naw, not that I can recollect," he answered. "Some dimwits from down 'round Ft. Walton was out there chasin' a pair of dolphins the other mornin.' I shot 'em for ya."

"I appreciate that, my friend. Nothing else, though?"

"No, can't say there has been," he said, staring at her curiously. "Whatcha lookin' for?"

"Well, Axel found a man's leg in his one of his nets this morning."

"Hellfire, you don't say," the old man said, shaking his head again. "Shark?"

"Nope."

"Propeller?"

"No, I'm afraid not."

"Wait'll Rae gets a load of this. They got *Murder, She Wrote* over on the Netflix now, you know. She's been watchin' the daylights out of it. She'll be tickled to death."

"Yeah, well, I'm glad she'll be happy," Maggie said, trying to smile.

Mel looked a bit more subdued and nodded his head. "Yeah, it's not exactly good for the tourist trade, I suppose."

"Not the tourists *we* want," Maggie said. "Well, listen, I'm gonna go down the dock, see if anybody's aboard."

"Well, you just missed your daddy, and Fred Carlton and his crew was here til about twenty minutes ago, but I don't think anyone else is around. Oystermen came in early today. Wicked hot. Shrimpers aren't here yet. Oh, wait! 'Cept David, he's down there with his new trawler."

"David got a new shrimp boat?" Maggie asked. She hadn't seen him since Grace's funeral, but he had her told a few weeks back that he almost had the money for a new boat.

"Yeah, he's right down there," Mel said, waving his arm down toward the other docks, closer to Boudreaux's business and the dock where the Sheriff's Office boat was moored. "Got himself a nice old Jefferson."

"Okay, Mel, thanks." Maggie gave him a half-hearted wave, then went back to her Jeep. She drove the city block to a small public parking area next to Sea-Fair, and headed down toward the last docks, where most of the shrimp boats moored.

Halfway there, she spotted David's new boat, and David on the deck winding a new rope onto the winch. He was wearing old jeans and a stained white tee shirt, and his onyx-black hair shone in the sunlight as he bent over the winch.

Maggie stopped on the dock, on his starboard side, and took a look at the boat. The royal blue paint on the hull was chipped and peeling, but the nets looked new, and so did the doors, the rectangular pieces of wood attached to the nets to keep them just above, but not dragging on, the bottom of the sea floor.

Maggie watched him winding the stiff, white rope onto the winch and felt a moment of pride and gratitude. Just before the BP spill, David had taken a loan on a new shrimp boat. He'd lost it a few months after the spill and had spent the next several month doing odd jobs, crewing for the few shrimpers who could still afford a paid crew, and beginning a new drinking career.

A year after the spill, he was transporting pot for a cousin of his that grew it in Tate's Hell Forest and Maggie had asked him to leave. It was now five years since their divorce, but they'd been together since they were ten years old, and he would always be the best friend she'd ever had.

Maggie swallowed hard at the memory of all the years she had watched him get ready to head out to the bay, then cleared her throat.

"Hey," she said.

He looked up and smiled, his green eyes startling in between his black bangs and close-cut beard.

"Hey, baby! What do you think?"

"It's beautiful," she said. They'd both always had a thing for the older boats.

David hitched up his jeans and stuffed his hands into his front pockets. "Well, I had to replace the nets and chains and doors, and it needs paint and a lot of topside work, but I think it's gonna be a fine boat eventually," he said.

"When did you get it?"

"Just got back from Mobile this morning. That guy I rebuilt the motor for, he gave me a good deal. Cash."

"This is great, David. I'm really happy for you."

"Me, too, babe." He shrugged self-consciously. "I'm gonna get my life back. Not all of it, maybe, but the 'me' part."

Maggie nodded. "What about the other thing?"

"I'm out, Maggie. Done."

"The kids are going to be really proud of you, David," Maggie said, blinking away tears. "I'm proud of you."

"Thanks. I've gotta get a crew, but Axel's gonna go out with me tonight and I talked to Mike last week. Things are tight and he said he'll crew for me again. He says he knows a couple of good guys who might come out a few nights."

Maggie nodded again and smiled. "You'll get there."

"Yeah." They looked at each other a moment, both with different memories of a different time. "So, what are you doing over here?"

Maggie shook her head and looked around the docks. "I was hoping to catch some more people down here. Did Axel tell you what happened this morning?"

"No, I figured he was asleep when I got back, so I haven't called him today. Is he okay?"

"Yeah, but he got a human foot in his net. A leg, really."

"Are you serious?"

"Yeah, and no, it wasn't a shark."

David ran a hand through his hair, which had grown out quite a bit and was damp where it touched the base of his neck. "Geez, I leave town for a week and all of a sudden we're living in Twin Peaks."

"Yeah, well. I guess it'll keep me employed."

David wiped at his forehead, then hopped up on the gangway and to the dock.

"I've gotta walk over to the soda machine. Want to walk with me?"

"Sure."

"How are the kids?" David asked as they walked toward the Sea-Fair office.

"They're good. You should call them."

"I will. I'll call them before I go out. So what do you think is up with this leg or foot or whatever?"

"No clue."

"Well, if I drag any parts up tonight, I'm chucking 'em back," he said.

Maggie smiled at him. "Just weight them down first and mark them with a buoy for me, okay?"

"Will do." They walked in silence for a moment, just the crunching of oyster shells below and the rasping of palm fronds above to break the quiet. "So, how's Wyatt?"

David had known Maggie was getting involved with Wyatt before she'd known it for sure herself. He'd taken it well, though she knew he'd been hurt.

"He's okay," she said, uncomfortable. "We haven't...we haven't gone on a date or anything yet."

David nodded without looking at her.

They reached the main building, and stopped at the old RC Cola machine. David dug into his pocket for change. He looked at her and smiled. "How about an RC, baby?"

"Sure," Maggie said with half a smile.

He started loading change into the machine. "You remember when we used to sneak down here, grab some RCs and go make out on your Dad's skiff?"

Maggie smiled. "Yeah. I also remember the night those Donnelly boys tried to steal Vern Burwell's trawler, and we ended up surrounded by PD."

David grinned. "Aw, man, that sucked. I thought Gray was gonna kill me. I spent an hour listening to him tell me about your virtue. It took me another hour to convince him I hadn't taken it."

He got two sodas, popped hers open and handed it to her.

"Thanks," she said, and took a sip. She watched him open his soda and dip his head back for a long swallow, saw the spot near his Adam's apple that she had always loved to kiss, and her chest hurt, but it was a mild ache.

"You should find someone, David," she said softly.

He took another drink, then looked at her for a moment. "I will one of these days, Maggie. I'm still letting go of us."

Maggie looked down at her brown hiking boots, the frayed bottoms of her jeans.

"Hey," David said, and she looked up at him. "It's okay. I know it's too little too late."

"I'm sorry."

"Me, too. " He took a deep breath and let it out with a smile. "But things are looking up."

"Yes." Maggie nodded and smiled. "I've got to go. I'm glad you're home."

David opened his arms, and Maggie leaned in and wrapped her arms around his waist, her head coming to rest where it always had, just beneath his neck.

"I love you, David."

"I love you too, babe."

Maggie stepped back and gave him a half wave.

"Take care," he said to her.

"You too," she answered, then turned and headed for her car. When she got into the Jeep and looked, David was walking back to his new boat. She almost jumped back out of the Jeep to yell, "Break the nets," like she used to back when they were married and she would see him off with his dinner and his Thermos.

It was her version of "break a leg" and he'd always laughed about it. But somehow, it just seemed like it would almost be unkind to say it now.

CHAPTER
FOUR

aggie lived about five miles northwest of town, in a cypress stilt house built by her father's father back in the 1950s. The house was half a mile down a gravel road, and sat on a spit of land that curved out into the river, so that there was river on two sides of the house. She had no near neighbors. The house was surrounded by woods and her gravel road was at the dead end of the road that led out of town.

She stopped at the mailbox on Bluff Road, then turned onto the gravel, thankful for the instant shade from the trees on either side. Eventually, she pulled into the wide front yard area, more gravel and dirt than grass, and parked. Maggie's Catahoula Parish Leopard Hound, Coco, was halfway down the stairs from the wraparound deck by the time Maggie turned off the Jeep.

Coco came at Maggie from the stairs and Maggie's one Americana Rooster, Stoopid, flailed across the parking area from the other side. Dog and bird converged a few feet in front of Maggie as she shut the door, then Stoopid veered off and did one of his figure-eight maneuvers before running back toward the chicken yard. Coco commenced a full-on emotional arrest and threw herself at Maggie's legs.

"Hey, baby," Maggie said, and knelt down to kiss Coco's face and rub her neck. "How's my girl?"

Coco was too overjoyed to answer, but danced alongside Maggie as she made her way to the house. Coco's tags jingled behind Maggie as she climbed the stairs, pulled her boots off with her feet, and walked into the house.

The front door opened immediately onto their dining area, and Maggie dropped her purse and keys on the old table just a few feet from the door. Her ten-year old son, Kyle, the spitting image of his father, was on the couch playing Minecraft.

"Hey, Buddy," Maggie said.

Kyle looked up at her and smiled wide, looked at her with David's green eyes and thick, dark lashes. "Hey, Mom! You gotta see this new mod I got."

Maggie leaned down to kiss his forehead. "Show me in a little bit, okay? I've got to start dinner. Did your sister take the chicken out?"

"I don't know," he answered, already focusing back on the TV. "We just got back a little while ago."

Maggie walked into the kitchen, an ell open to the dining area and living room. She walked to the old cast iron farm sink, rescued from the house where her grandma had grown up, and looked in. There were a few cups, but no chicken. Maggie sighed and walked to the hallway off of the living room.

"Sky!" she called, then walked back to the kitchen and opened the fridge. She heard Sky's bedroom door open, and Sky appeared beside her a moment later, earbuds in and phone in hand.

"Hey," she said.

Maggie looked up and pointed at her own ear. Sky took one of the earbuds out. Maggie could hear music she hated, tinny and small.

"You forgot to take the chicken out to thaw."

"Oh. Sorry."

Sky was beautiful when she wasn't sullen. She looked more like her mom than her dad. Although her green eyes could have belonged to either parent, she had Maggie's long, dark brown hair, full lips and strong chin.

Maggie sighed. "Sky, I just asked you to do one thing, hon."

"I'm sorry," Sky said defensively. "We were running late for Kyle's friend's dumb birthday party and I forgot."

Maggie threw a hand on her hip as she looked back into the fridge. She needed to go shopping, on someone else's schedule.

"Well, I guess it's grilled cheese and tomato soup," she said, and grabbed the cheese before closing the fridge.

"Sounds okay to me," Sky said. "I've lost my appetite after spending the whole day eating cupcakes and listening to ten year old nerds talk about Minecraft and Mario."

Maggie got a skillet out of the drawer beneath the oven and set it on the stove. "I just need you to help me out a little more while you guys are out of school, okay?"

"Yeah. Okay." She put her earbud in and headed out of the kitchen. "Call me when it's ready."

Maggie sliced some butter and dropped it into the pan, then turned on the gas burner. Then she walked out toward the living area.

"Has she been like this all day?" Maggie asked.

"I guess so," Kyle said to the TV.

"What's up with her?"

"Her-mones," he answered with a shrug.

"Awesome." Maggie walked back into the kitchen, thanking God she had some wine in the house.

⚓ ⚓ ⚓

Bennett Boudreaux drank the last few sips of his first cup of chicory coffee, then poured another cup before starting to unwrap the newspaper. Amelia, the tall, rangy, middle-aged Creole woman who cooked and cleaned for him, was cooking some bacon and eggs on the cooktop in the kitchen island, and the smell was getting to him.

After years of oystering before he built his businesses, the only solid food he could stomach first thing in the morning was raw oysters. But Miss Evangeline, Amelia's ninety-something year old mother, would be along shortly and require one over-medium egg, one slice of dark toast, one slice of crisp bacon, and a cup of tea.

Miss Evangeline had been his father's housekeeper/ nanny back in Houma, LA, but he'd left her behind when they'd moved to Apalachicola. When Bennett had graduated college and gone back to Houma to expand his father's shrimp business and build his own, he'd hired her back, and Amelia with her. When his father had died and Bennett had moved back to Apalach, he'd brought them both along, much to his wife's displeasure, which had been part of the appeal. Now they lived out back in the guesthouse, and Amelia took care of the house while Miss Evangeline slung voodoo around and ate the mangoes Bennett grew just for her.

He opened the paper and the headline smacked him in the face. Apparently, a piece of Brandon "Sport" Wilmette had found its way into a shrimper's net.

He skimmed the article quickly. They didn't know yet who the owner of the foot was, how it had come to be in the ocean, or when, but Bennett doubted that anyone other than him had recently cut anyone's throat, chopped him up and chucked him out into the water.

Sport had come to him after his nephew Gregory's funeral last week. He'd thought he would surprise Bennett with the news that, twenty-two years ago, Gregory had raped Maggie Redmond, but Gregory had already told Bennett, the night before his body was found on the beach, declared dead from a self-inflicted gunshot to the mealy mouth.

What *did* surprise Bennett was Sport's admission that he had been a witness to the rape, albeit an inactive one, and his suspicion that Maggie had actually killed Gregory and made it look like a suicide.

Less surprising was Sport's foolhardy attempt to blackmail Bennett over the rape, to protect the family's tenuous grip on good public relations. Bennett had cut his throat for being a blackmailer, and a sorry excuse for a gentleman besides.

He saw, as he concluded his reading of the article, that Maggie was investigating Sport's foot. That was a bit troublesome, but nothing to get too concerned about; he could handle Maggie.

The back door opened, and Miss Evangeline's walker banged into each door jamb with an aluminum tap before preceding her into the room.

"Mornin', Mama," Amelia said from the stove as she plated her mother's breakfast.

"So it seem," Miss Evangeline said in her raspy voice.

Bennett stood and walked to Miss Evangeline's chair, pulled it out for her, and waited.

Miss Evangeline was not quite five feet tall and weighed less than a healthy tomcat. She'd once smacked Bennett with a wooden spoon when he was about twelve, for saying the red bandana on her head made her look like a paintbrush. She seemed to get smaller every year, and her little flowered housedresses got looser and longer.

"Good morning, Miss Evangeline," Bennett said, kissing both of her papery brown cheeks as she reached the table. "How are you this morning?"

"One my tenny ball go flat. Now my walky-talky all crooked, gon' dump me in the floor."

"I'll get you some more tennis balls," Bennett said and scooted her chair in for her easily once she'd sat. Then he walked back to his chair and sat down, as Amelia placed her mother's plate and tea in front of her.

"I got another can in the laundry room," Amelia said, and walked out of the kitchen toward the back of the house.

Bennett went back to his paper, as Miss Evangeline began her protracted morning ritual of buttering very square inch of her toast.

"This toast not hot," she said. She twisted her birdlike neck to look toward the stove, then peered across the table at Bennett.

"Where Amelia at?"

Bennett picked his paper back up and went back to the article.

"I sent her to out back to bury Lily," he said, speaking of his beloved wife. "She was done polishing the silver."

Miss Evangeline stared blankly at the back of Bennett's paper, then flipped her upper plate out with her tongue and got it resituated before she spoke.

"You gon' sass me some today, then."

"No, I was just responding to your query," Bennett said to the paper. "She went to get your tenny ball. I think you're starting to go senile on me."

"Go 'head mouth off to me some mo'. I buzz you with my buzzer."

Bennett lowered the paper to the table. "For the last time, it's not a 'buzzer.' It's not like one of those party tricks that gives somebody a little zap. It's a Taser. It's for self-defense, not for smacking someone you can't reach, and not for frying the brains out of the neighbor's dog."

Miss Evangeline sat up to her full three feet and made a little irritated sound in her throat. "Puppy don't need to be runnin' round Mr. Benny yard, poopin' his poop all 'round. Then nobody wanna go out there get my mango."

Bennett sighed and went back to his paper. Miss Evangeline occupied herself with the complicated maneuver of fork and knife for a moment, then looked back across the table.

"What in the paper?" she asked, nibbling a microscopic bit of egg.

Bennett spoke through the paper, while he finished reading the article. "Well, fortunately for you, something interesting for a change. Axel Blackwell found a foot in his net yesterday morning."

"Who Axel Blackwell?"

"A shrimper."

"Who foot?"

"They don't know yet," Bennett said.

Bennett continued reading while Miss Evangeline undertook the task of raising her teacup to her mouth and putting it back down.

"Juju got somebody," she said.

"Clearly," Bennett answered.

He was tempted to tell her that he had been the only agent of juju where Sport Wilmette was concerned, but he refrained.

She was awfully attached to her voodoo, and it would be embarrassing for the town gangster to get buzzed to hell and back by his two hundred year old nanny.

⚓ ⚓ ⚓

Maggie spent most of that day fielding calls from locals who saw the foot in the paper and had questions, complaints or vaguely-related suspicions or reports. Nothing came of any of it. Some of the calls came from vacationers out on the island, though not as many as locals seemed to fear. Most of them just wanted to know what to do with any miscellaneous parts that might wash up on the beach while they were grilling their hamburgers.

By the end of the day, Maggie was entirely weary of assuring people that there was no shark involved, and it took some effort not to mention that if they did find a shark who could use an ax or a knife, Apalach would have a whole different niche in the tourist industry.

She rolled her head to loosen up her neck, and was just about to go rummage through the break room fridge for a soda when her desk phone rang again. She sighed and picked it up.

"Franklin County Sheriff's Office, this is Lt. Redmond."

"Maggie?" a woman's voice asked.

"Yes, this is Maggie Redmond."

"It's Claire West from the Bayview."

The Bayview Inn was a hotel and restaurant on Water Street overlooking the marina. Maggie knew Claire only slightly; her son played on Kyle's softball team.

"Hi, Claire, what can I do for you?"

"Well, listen. I just got back from a little vacation down in Miami with my sister, and I just saw the paper."

"Okay."

"Well, I'm wondering if it might have anything to do with a guest that up and disappeared on us last week."

Maggie sat up a little straighter and forgot the crick in her neck.

"When last week?"

"I looked it up on the register. We went to clean his room last Wednesday morning and his stuff was there, but he was gone. It was just an overnight bag and I thought he might have just forgotten it, but he didn't pay for his last night, either."

"What's this guest's name?"

"It's right here. Brandon Wilmette, from Atlanta."

"Where are his things?"

"Luanne brought them to me last week and I just put them in the lost and found, in case he called or came back. I mean, it could be a misunderstanding. Or he may have had an emergency or something."

"Do you have a phone number for him?" Maggie asked, grabbing a pen and paper.

"Yes, it's 404-976-2339. Do you want me to call it?"

"No, I'll call it. Thanks, Claire. I'll call you or stop by if I need anything else, okay?"

"Okay, Maggie." Clair sighed. "Gee, I hope it's not him. That would just be creepy."

Maggie disconnected the call, then dialed the number Claire had given her. It went straight to voice mail.

"Hey, this is Sport. I'm doing something more interesting than answering the phone, so leave me a number and I'll probably call you back," a man's voice said snidely.

Maggie left her name and number and asked Brandon Wilmette to call her back, then hung up the phone and walked down the hallway to Wyatt's open door.

Wyatt was at his desk, using two fingers to peck at his keyboard.

"Hey," Maggie said. Wyatt looked up. "The Bayview Hotel just called. A guy named Wilmette never checked out last week, and never came back to get his stuff."

"You have a number for him?"

"Straight to voice mail. I'm gonna drive over there and take a look at his belongings, maybe get another number for him."

"I'll come with you," Wyatt said, looking at his watch. "It's time to leave anyway."

"Okay."

Wyatt got up and headed toward the door. "No gossiping, though. I have steaks to marinate."

CHAPTER
FIVE

Maggie and Wyatt found Claire polishing the silver-ware in the dining room of the hotel, one of many riverside warehouses and buildings left over from the years that Apalach had been one of the biggest cotton ports on the Gulf.

Claire hadn't remembered much about Brandon Wil-mette, just that she knew she'd checked him in and hadn't seen him much the couple of days he'd been there. She had a vague recollection that he might have been around forty, that he didn't say much, and that he smoked.

She took them into the linen room that also served as a lost and found, and left them there to look through Wil-mette's overnight bag, an expensive but worn brown leath-er case.

Wyatt unzipped the main compartment and pulled a ball of clothing out onto the small table. Maggie pulled the case closer to her and started going through the small-er compartments.

"Snazzy dresser," Wyatt said, holding up a wrinkled teal blazer that was made out of a too-shiny material. He started going through the pockets.

Maggie pulled out a small handful of papers. A boarding pass from Delta, flight 880, which brought him to Panama City at 11:14 a.m. Saturday before last. Wednesday morning he was gone.

"He flew into Northwest on Saturday the 20th," Maggie said. "I wonder if someone drove him down here or he rented a car."

"We'll have to ask Claire." Wyatt held up a crumpled receipt. "He went to Caroline's on Sunday. Twenty-six dollar tab and he left a two dollar tip."

"Nice." Maggie pulled another receipt out of the handful of papers. It was from the flower shop on Commerce Street, from Monday the 23rd. "He spent eighty-eight on flowers at The Blooming Idiot. Maybe he was willing to spend for the right reasons."

"Maybe a woman."

"Yeah." Maggie pulled out her phone and called the number on the receipt. She got the answering machine and hung up. "They're already closed. I'll stop by there on my way to work in the morning."

"I got nothing else," Wyatt said, running his hand along the bottom of the main compartment. "You don't have a rental car agreement in there or anything?"

"Nope. But it could be in the car." Maggie tucked the papers back into their zippered compartment. The other one on the opposite side was empty, save for a pocket comb. She gently pulled it out and held it up to the light. "No hairs."

"Too bad."

"Yeah." Maggie put it back. "We could probably find some on that jacket, though."

"Well, first let's see if we can make sure this guy didn't just max out his card on heavy tipping and skip out on his room. I'll call Atlanta in the morning."

"I'm sorry about that."

"Me, too. Love those guys. Nice Muzak."

After returning Wilmette's bag to the shelf where it had been stored, Maggie and Wyatt found Claire in the lobby and asked about a car. After pulling his check-in information from the computer, Claire gave them the tag number for a rented blue Kia Sedona.

A quick look around the hotel parking lot determined that the car was as gone as Wilmette. Maggie and Wyatt walked back toward their cars.

"I'll call Jeff on my way home," said Wyatt, referring to their IT guy. "Have him run the plates, call the rental car company."

"Okay. I'm gonna go home and take a shower."

"I appreciate that."

"What are you saying?"

"Well, it's just an indication that you're putting forth some effort for our date. I intend to shower as well."

Maggie tossed him a grin and looked at her watch. "It's almost six. What time to do you want me over there?"

"Whenever you've dried off."

"I'm taking the kids over to my parents for dinner and a movie," Maggie said, opening her Jeep door. "Seven okay?"

"Sounds good." Wyatt opened his own door and looked at her over the roof of his cruiser. "Are you nervous?"

"A little. You?"

"I'm a little stressed about the marinade," he said. "By the way, I'm a man and I eat man food, so if you want a vegetable, eat it before you come over."

Maggie pulled onto her parent's property shortly before seven. They lived in an older house out on 98, just before the Apalach city limits. The back yard ran right up to the bay, and her folks had bought it back when middle class folks could afford it.

Maggie drove to the end of the long gravel driveway and parked, but left the motor running. She popped the trunk as Sky got out of the passenger seat, Kyle got out of the back, and Maggie's mom, Georgia, came out onto the front porch.

"Look at you," Georgia said, smiling.

Maggie had gone through an extraordinary amount of angst choosing something to wear. She'd finally settled on a long blue skirt with little white flowers on it, a white tank top and sandals. For other women, this would have been something to wear to the grocery store. For Maggie, it was dressing up.

She shrugged a little and tried to smile. "Is it too much?"

"No, sweetie, you look great. He's grilling, right?"

"Yeah," Maggie said, as the kids got their backpacks out of the trunk and came around to the front of the car.

"Then it's just right," Georgia said, and Maggie decided to believe her. Her mom had always been a beautiful woman, but beautiful without trying to be. At fifty-eight, she still turned heads.

Maggie's father, Gray, came out onto the porch.

"Hey, y'all," he said with a big smile. He was almost as tall as Wyatt, but much thinner. He was a strong man, having worked the oyster beds all his life, but he'd had lung cancer a couple of years before and was still trying to gain some weight, though he'd never been stout.

"Hey there, Sunshine," he said to Maggie. "I don't remember the last time I saw you in a dress."

"It's a skirt," she said self-consciously.

"It has no legs," he said.

"Leave her alone, Gray. She's nervous," Georgia said.

"Nervous? What for? She's beautiful," Gray said.

"It's their first date."

"No it isn't. They came over here for dinner and Scrabble just a couple weeks ago."

"Omigosh, Granddad, that wasn't a date," Sky said, hoisting her backpack higher on her shoulder. "That was them serving you notice."

"Well, I noticed," Gray said.

"You guys, shut up," Maggie said. "Kyle, did you remember your toothbrush?'

"Yep," Kyle said, but he was focused on an Android game.

"Are they spending the night?" Gray asked.

"I told you that this morning, Gray," Georgia said. "Come on, kids, I made you some barbecued chicken."

Maggie kissed and hugged Kyle, then opened her arms for Sky. She was relieved when Sky leaned in for a hug, despite her sour mood earlier.

"Have fun with Wyatt Earp, Mom," she said with a grin.

"Ugh. So snotty," Maggie said.

"Dude. I told you, I like him. He's hot," Sky said as she headed into the house.

That left Maggie standing there by her open door and Gray standing on the porch with his hands in his pockets. They looked at each other a moment.

"Are you figuring you'll be out late, hon?" he asked.

"Not really," Maggie answered. "Mom wanted the kids to stay."

Gray nodded. "Well, have a good time, Sunshine. Maybe I'll stop by there later, see how things are going."

"Dad."

"Okay, we'll kid around later, then."

⚓ ⚓ ⚓

Maggie sat in the driveway of Wyatt's sage green cottage, just off Lafayette Park, in a neighborhood that was part working-class and part historic district. She'd gotten there two minutes prior, but had stalled by checking what little makeup she wore, adjusting the air that wasn't on, and blowing into her hand to smell her breath.

Her personal cell phone rang on the console, and she answered without looking. "Hello?"

"Would you like me to bring your steak out to the driveway?"

Maggie sighed. "I'm coming."

"The door's open," Wyatt said.

"I don't think anyone should see me just opening your door."

"Well, I don't think anyone should see me opening it *for* you in my boxers."

Maggie felt a twinge of alarm. This was her boss. Her friend. "Why are you in your boxers?"

"Because I am not yet in my pants. Are you coming or not?"

"Don't you have a robe?"

"No, I don't have a robe," he answered indignantly. Maggie could hear him struggling with something.

"Why not?"

"Because I'm not eighty-three years old."

"Geez, Wyatt. You don't have to get snappy," she snapped.

Twenty feet away, Wyatt opened his front door, his phone to his ear

"There," he said through the phone. "Now the neighbors can see that I opened the door for you and that I'm wearing pants."

Maggie disconnected the call and took a deep breath, then got out of the Jeep and headed up the driveway. Wyatt was wearing khaki pants and a white button down shirt, untucked, with the sleeves rolled up. Chest hair peeked out above the first fastened button and his wavy brown hair was still a bit damp. As she walked toward the front door, it occurred to Maggie that, aside from the fact that he was a good man, everything about Wyatt was completely different from David.

Maggie stopped at the top step and watched him look at her.

"You're wearing a skirt," he said.

"So everybody says," she said, managing a smile.

He took in her dark brown hair, loose and curling around her shoulders, the touch of makeup. "You look really nice," he said quietly.

"So do you," she said.

They looked at each other a moment, then he seemed to remember where they were. He stepped back. "Come on in."

Maggie walked into the living room, cozily furnished with rattan furniture, a turquoise surfboard propped up in one corner. It was a surprisingly warm room for a single man. Maggie had only been there once before, but she'd been too nervous to notice, really.

"Let's go out back," Wyatt said, as he shut the door.

Maggie followed him through the living room and into the kitchen/dining area. An open pair of French doors made up the back wall, and Maggie could see the bay just beyond his back yard. Wyatt walked out onto a covered back patio and Maggie followed.

It was just thinking about becoming dusk, and the palm trees, on either side of the house and throughout the yard, rustled with the evening breeze. Eight-foot tall hibiscus hedges shielded the back yard from the neighbors on either side.

There was a large stainless grill at one end of the patio. Two large ribeye steaks sat on a built-in cutting board. Maggie hadn't realized she was hungry until that moment. There was a table and four chairs near the grill, a few other chairs scattered about, and at the opposite end of the patio hung a white porch swing.

Wyatt stopped at the table and opened a bottle of deep red wine, poured some into the two glasses waiting there. "So, I was working on a plan while I was in the shower."

He held a glass out to her, and she stepped over to the table to take it, gratefully.

"A plan for what?"

"For getting through the first five minutes of our first date."

Maggie chewed the corner of her lip. "What do you mean?"

"Take a big gulp of that wine first," he said, and took his own advice. Maggie did as instructed and felt the warmth move down her throat and into her stomach.

"See, we've got all the usual first date uncertainty stuff, but we've also got the fact that we've been together nearly every day for about six years. That we work together."

"Okay." Maggie took another healthy swallow.

"So, on the one hand, we know each other really well," Wyatt continued. "You've watched me move out of the grieving process with my wife. I've watched you go through it with David. We've handled some pretty scary cases together. I've damn near died of a stroke seeing you lying under the body of a dead tweaker who'd been about to blow your face off."

Maggie detected a whiff of cordite and meth sweat in the air, chose to ignore it. "Yes," she said.

"We've had our year or so of playful flirtation, and we even had our first kiss, which I have to say was exceptional, and now here we are and we're actually going to pursue this thing."

Maggie swallowed hard.

"Right?" he asked.

"Right," Maggie said, nodding.

"So let's get all of that first date weirdness out of the way right off the bat so we can actually relax and enjoy ourselves."

"Which weirdness?' Maggie asked, as Wyatt set down his wine and reached out and took hers, too.

"Well, for instance, let's check this out," he said, and took her hand and led her over to the swing.

He held out a hand, indicating she should sit, so she did. He sat down next to her, very close, and put an arm around her shoulder.

"Okay, so this is what this is like," he said. "You're still comically short, but you feel really good, and my arm is probably heavy, but I bet I smell good."

"You do."

"I put it on special, just for you," he said, wagging his brows at her, and his face was so close that she could see gold beams radiating out from the pupils of his brown eyes.

She was just about to need to kiss him when he grabbed her hand and stood up again. He pulled her to him, wrapped his arms around her.

"And this is us doing this," he said, and his chest was hard and seemed to go upward forever. His voice rumbled through her chest and his thighs were warm against her waist.

"This is nice," she managed to say into his shirt.

"Yes. Yes, it is," he said. "And now I don't have to wonder what it will feel like if your boobs actually touch me, and I can focus on having witty conversation."

Maggie swallowed hard and was suddenly extremely conscious of the fact that she had breasts. Wyatt bent his head and gently buried his nose in her hair.

"And now I know what your hair smells like," he said more quietly.

"Does it smell good?" she asked, for something to say.

"Yes."

After a moment, wherein she breathed in the scents of fresh cotton and bar soap, Wyatt bent back a little and she looked up into his face.

"See, now we can go ahead and get that second kiss over with," Wyatt said, and his face was more serious. "Then we don't have to waste all night wondering if we should do it, or when, or what it'll be like the second time."

"We should," Maggie said, and Wyatt bent down and put his mouth on hers.

She remembered him instantly. She remembered the way he had felt and tasted the first time, and this kiss was partly a return and partly a venturing further into something completely new, something that wasn't a test, but a testament. It was sweet and it was commanding, it was gentle and it was firm, it was new but it was immediately recognizable as right.

It was, she realized, exactly what and who she wanted.

When Wyatt finally straightened up and looked at her, his eyes were serious and frank, but then the familiar twinkle returned.

"Now that we've got all that worked out, how do you like your steak?"

Maggie smiled, partly in relief. "I don't actually require that you cook it at all."

Wyatt kissed her forehead and let go of her, made his way to the grill. "My kind of woman," he said. "But let's put on a show, just to be socially acceptable."

He slapped the steaks onto the grill. The sizzle and the aromas of beef, Balsamic vinegar, and garlic made Maggie's stomach clench. She was starving. She drained half her wine as a consolation.

After the fewest possible minutes of actual cookery, Wyatt placed the steaks on two plates and set them on the table, where two places had been laid.

"Oh, I forgot the bread," Wyatt said, and hurried into the kitchen. Maggie sat down at her place and breathed in the steak, until he returned with a loaf of toasted Cuban bread and some butter.

He set them down in the middle of the table, then sat. They looked at each other a moment.

"I should have bought candles," he said.

"This is fine."

"Next time," he said.

"Next time's at my house," Maggie said, and Wyatt smiled.

"No vegetables," he said.

⚓ ⚓ ⚓

After they finished eating, Wyatt and Maggie spent the next several hours laughing, talking, and trying out various positions indicating togetherness. Maggie grew accustomed to the feel of Wyatt's chest as he sat behind her on the end of his dock, and how much larger his hand was than hers. Wyatt began to find the scent of gardenias on her neck familiar, and had finally been able to relax around her boobs, which were normally safely encased in a Sheriff's Department polo.

They talked about work, then remembered they were on a date, and talked about his moving from Virginia to Cocoa Beach, after his wife's death from cancer. They talked about severed legs and then backtracked to her going out with her daddy on his oyster skiff as a child. They discussed missing rental cars and first-time sex, agitated paper editors and puberty. They talked about his disappointment in being left childless, and her struggles to raise her kids on her own.

By the time they stretched out their cramped muscles and he took her hand to walk her to the door, they had transitioned full circle from familiarity to newness and back again, only the familiarity itself was a new one.

They both stopped at the breakfast bar, drained the last of their wine, and set the glasses down. When Maggie looked up, Wyatt was smiling at her.

"What?" she asked, smiling back.

"Look how far you've come since the last time you were here."

"That was like two weeks ago."

"Yes, and at that time you'd only kissed the guy you'd loved since infancy—"

"Fifth grade."

"—whenever, and the gay guy from State Farm."

"I told you, that was truth or dare. And I don't think he knew he was gay then."

"Be that as it may, now here we are."

"Where's that?" she asked.

"Somewhere else," he said, and he'd stopped smiling.

He held out his hand and she took it, then he started walking her toward the door again.

"Wyatt, aren't you just a little bit worried about it?" Maggie asked. "I mean, our jobs...and then, we've had this great working relationship and friendship. Aren't you worried about losing at least one of those things?"

They stopped at the door and Maggie leaned up against the wall.

"No, I'm not," he said.

"Why not?"

"Because I have you to do that for me." He put his hand on the wall beside her head. "And you're doing a great job."

CHAPTER

SIX

T he next morning, after fewer than four hours sleep, Maggie stopped at Café Con Leche on Water Street and got a double café to go, then drove around the corner to the florist on Commerce.

When she walked in, she found a very thin blond man in his fifties behind the register. Maggie couldn't remember his name, but she recognized both him and his partner, a larger, slightly younger man with black hair and startling gray eyes, who was wiping down a butcher block counter behind the register.

"Good morning!" the blond man sang out in a soft, smoky voice and Maggie remembered that his name was William.

"Good morning," Maggie said, smiling politely. She walked up to the front counter. "I'm Lt. Redmond from the Sheriff's Office."

"Yes, I see," William said, raising his eyebrows at her blue polo shirt. "How can I help you?"

Maggie pulled the receipt out of her pocket and handed it to him as the dark-haired man came to peer over his shoulder.

"Can you look up this purchase? Or do you remember the man that made it?" she asked.

William read the receipt with a *hmm*, then looked over his shoulder at his partner. "Do you remember this one, Robert?"

"No, I don't think so," Robert said. "Let me look up the transaction number."

He stepped over to a desktop computer on the back counter and started typing.

"Can you believe it's this wicked hot at eight o' clock in the morning?" William asked Maggie. "I stepped out on our balcony before sunrise and almost withered away."

"It is unusually hot," Maggie agreed.

"If we could just get a good rain, right?" William asked. "I mean, what the hell? It's hurricane season, for Pete's sake."

"Oh!" Robert said, looking over his shoulder. "It's Sonny Crocket."

"Oh, him!" William said and shook his head at Maggie. "You just don't know. Straight off the set of *Miami Vice*. I thought maybe a Delorean had crashed out front."

Robert came back to the counter with a printed copy of the transaction. "Except his name was Wilmette. Remember, from Atlanta?"

"Right, Atlanta. Dumber than dirt, as well."

"Bless his heart," Robert said.

"Why?" Maggie asked.

"I don't think he knows he's gay," William said conspiratorially.

"Well, clearly, otherwise he'd dress like he had some sense," Robert said.

"Is he in trouble?" William asked.

"Well, no. We're looking for him," Maggie said. She craned her neck to look at the printout. "Does it say what he purchased?"

"Oh, I remember it," William said. "He got a wreath."

"A wreath?" Maggie asked.

"Yeah, he was down for a funeral," Robert said.

"Whose?"

"Bennett Boudreaux's nephew, the one that shot himself," William said.

Maggie stopped breathing for a moment.

"Are you sure?" she asked quietly.

"Yeah, we sent it to the cemetery," Robert said.

"So why are you looking for him?" William asked, his voice hushed, although no one else was in the store.

"We just need to ask him about something," Maggie said. "Do you recall him saying anything about how long he was here for?"

William looked at Robert before shaking his head.

"Do you remember what he was driving?"

"Actually, he walked," William said. "I know, because I went out for a smoke while Robert was ringing him up. He was just staying over at the Bayview. I noticed he was on foot."

"The foot!" Robert gasped. "Is he the foot?"

"No, no, we're just trying to find him," Maggie said.

"We don't like the foot," William said.

Robert shook his head. "The foot is bad for business."

Maggie nodded and smiled, although she felt a little sick to her stomach. The mention of Gregory Boudreaux had been doing that to her lately.

"Okay, well, if you remember anything else about him, give me a call, would you?" Maggie handed William her card.

"Sure. Of course," William said. As Maggie headed for the door, she heard him add, "I told you no good would come of that foot."

Maggie walked back out into the heat, grabbed her coffee out of the console of her Jeep, and stood there drinking it while she let the car air out.

They'd found Gregory Boudreaux's body on the beach on St. George Island, with a .38 gunshot wound to the mouth. Maggie was, unfortunately for her, the only investigator available at the moment. Unfortunate, because she had never told a soul that Gregory had raped her in the woods one day, when she was fifteen and he was home from college.

Larry had deemed the death a suicide and that should have been that. But Maggie's nightmares had started up again and the case had brought her and Bennett Boudreaux together in some strange sort of dance around the truth. He'd let her understand that he knew about the rape, though he hadn't actually come right out and said it. She'd also gotten the feeling that he suspected her of finally killing Gregory for it. What she didn't know was what he intended to do with that suspicion.

She also didn't know who had mailed her an apology from Gregory a few days after his funeral. An apology that had his fingerprints all over it. Had this guy Wilmette mailed it? Was he the other, unseen person who had been with Gregory when Gregory had come upon Maggie fishing all alone?

She'd been thinking that Wilmette was just the hapless owner of an unwelcome foot. Now he was all tied up with Gregory Boudreaux and things were getting messy.

After going back to the Bayview to look through Wilmette's things again, driving around to look fruitlessly for a blue Kia Sedona, and making the rounds at the marina, where no one reported seeing anything helpful, Maggie drove across the bridge to the office in Eastpoint.

She ducked her head into Wyatt's office on the way to her own, but while his desk looked to be in use, Wyatt wasn't at it. She waved or said hello to a few deputies on her way down the hall to her office, set her afternoon coffee on her desk, and sat down at her computer.

While her computer booted, Maggie had a sudden flash of memory that made the hairs stand up on her arms. Gregory Boudreaux, straddling her on the ground, atop a sheet of molding leaves, and looking off to the left somewhere in the woods.

Hey, you want some?

Maggie jumped a little when her computer beeped at her for her password, then she typed it in and pulled up arrest records. There were none for Brandon Wilmette, but there were several speeding tickets and DUIs, and she stared at the sullen Georgia State driver's license picture. Longish blond bangs tossed to one side. Dull hazel eyes. An Abercrombie T-shirt underneath a brown leather jacket. She didn't know him.

"Hey, I have interesting news to convey," said Wyatt cheerfully, as he walked into her office with an enormous Mountain Dew.

"Yeah, me too," Maggie said, less cheerfully.

"Me first. My buddy in Tallahassee called a few minutes ago. We got a hit on CODIS, thanks to a paternity suit from 2012. Our foot belongs to Brandon Wilmette. The baby, apparently, did not."

Maggie looked at him, as a heavy weight settled in her chest.

"Ta da," Wyatt said weakly. "You're not as excited by all this timesaving news as I wanted you to be."

"Yeah, well." Maggie flicked her pen a few times. "It would seem that Brandon Wilmette wasn't some tourist. He was here for Gregory Boudreaux's funeral."

"How'd you find that out?"

"I stopped by the flower shop."

"Huh." Wyatt folded himself into the metal chair in front of her desk and took a drink of his Mountain Dew. "Huh," he said again.

He looked at Maggie, but she didn't want to look him in the eye at the moment, so she stared at her pen.

"So what's your plan?" he asked.

"Well," she said, finally looking up. "I guess I'm going to go talk to Bennett Boudreaux."

Wyatt smiled. "Ah, yes, Uncle Bennett. Your new buddy and Cajun jitterbug partner."

"He's not my buddy," Maggie said half-heartedly. "But he can probably tell us something about Wilmette."

Wyatt regarded her for a moment and Maggie stared back at him until she became uncomfortable with it.

"What?" she asked.

"You and Boudreaux. It's problematic."

Maggie knew that, but she asked anyway. "In what way?"

"Well, first you're seen sucking down oysters with him at Boss Oyster—"

"That was work."

"I know that. Then you're dancing with him at the Cajun festival—"

"That was relief from work."

"I know that, too."

"He danced with a lot of respectable women."

"Nevertheless, all this has raised a few eyebrows," Wyatt said mildly. "Some people think Boudreaux has his heart set on having you in his pocket, since Bellows is now playing shuffleboard down in the Keys."

Gordon Bellows had been Maggie's predecessor, and was generally known to have been on Boudreaux's payroll, though nothing was ever proven.

"He's not trying to get me in his pocket."

"How do you know?"

"I asked him."

"Well. That's a nice, frank relationship you guys have going so far."

"It's really not a relationship, Wyatt." Maggie didn't care to mention that she'd also gone to Boudreaux to try to get help for Grace Carpenter, or that Boudreaux had actually tried to give it.

"Well, let's be clear," Wyatt said. He leaned over to peek out into the hallway before he spoke again, more softly. "I'm not worried about competition from a sixty-something year old man, but I am worried that he's after something."

"He seems to like me for some reason," Maggie said.

"Oh, that I don't doubt," Wyatt said. "But I don't think Boudreaux does anything simply because he likes, or even dislikes, someone. No disrespect to your charms, but he wants something."

Maggie looked back down at her desk. Wyatt was right, of course, but she wasn't able to tell Wyatt any of the reasons that he might be correct. She hadn't told him about her connection to Gregory, although she should have done so the minute they found hm on the beach. But she'd never told anyone, not even her parents. Not even David. Now it seemed too late to do that.

So, she couldn't tell Wyatt that she thought Boudreaux suspected her of killing Gregory, or that maybe he intended to repay her for it, or to use it against her as leverage in some way. She'd just have to leave Wyatt in the dark, and she was feeling increasingly bad, and increasingly worried, about that.

It also bothered her that she was starting to like Boudreaux enough to hope that he just liked her, despite what he knew and what he might suspect. It bothered her that she liked him at all.

Maggie looked back up at Wyatt, who was still watching her. "Well, I'm going to go talk to him."

"Maybe I should go, too."

"No. I think he'll speak more freely if it's just me," Maggie said. "We do have some kind of weird honesty thing going on."

Wyatt looked at her for a minute, then took a swig of his soda. "Okay. But if we pull one single case this year that *doesn't* have something to do with Boudreaux, I think you should start distancing yourself."

Maggie nodded, but she wondered if she meant it, exactly.

Bennett Boudreaux lived in a large but unassuming white frame house in the Historic District. Although the property took up almost an entire city lot and was owned by the richest man in town, it was curiously lacking in pomp and arrogance.

A wide porch wrapped around the entire house, with hanging baskets of flowers spaced periodically between the white wicker chairs and rockers, and the yard was filled with bougainvillea, hibiscus, and hydrangea in every conceivable color.

Maggie pulled into the oyster shell driveway behind Bennett's gray Mercedes S-class and turned off the engine. She saw Amelia look up from where she was sweeping the porch, then go back to her work. Maggie walked up to the porch and climbed the three wide, brick steps.

"Good afternoon," she said. "It's Amelia, isn't it?"

Amelia gave her just a glance, not sullen, exactly, but clearly disinterested. "Yes," she said, then went back to sweeping.

"Is Mr. Boudreaux at home? His office said he wasn't in today."

Amelia didn't stop sweeping, but she slowed up a bit. "Mr. Boudreaux on the back porch."

Maggie pointed beyond Amelia to the corner of the porch. "That way?"

"Yes."

"Thank you," Maggie said, then walked past the tall, cocoa-colored woman in the plumeria-covered housedress.

Her hiking boots clumped along the gray-painted wood planks of the porch as she made her way past more white furniture, more hanging flowers. Huge, twelve-pane windows revealed glimpses of ship's lathe walls and overstuffed, floral furniture. Much more feminine than Maggie would have assumed for Boudreaux, but then she remembered he had a fancy wife.

As she closed in on the back of the house, Maggie could hear Boudreaux speaking. When she rounded the corner, she saw him standing at a small white wrought-iron table. Seated at the table was the smallest, oldest woman Maggie had ever seen, and she realized that this must be Amelia's mother, the one few people had seen in the last couple of decades.

The little woman looked up as Maggie approached, her eyes enormous behind Coke bottle glasses. She wore a yellow bandana on her head and a faded, flowered housedress much like her daughter's.

Boudreaux looked over his shoulder at Maggie and smiled. She was struck again by how handsome he was. He wasn't over five foot seven or eight, but he was trim in his khaki trousers and lilac cotton shirt, and there was just a touch of silver in his full head of thick, golden-brown hair. But mostly, it was the eyes. They were the bluest eyes Maggie had ever seen, and he had a way of looking so intently at someone that it was like being pinned to a corkboard and examined.

"Well, hello, Maggie," Boudreaux said as she approached.

"Hello, Mr. Boudreaux," Maggie answered. Boudreaux was peeling one of several different types of mango on a cutting board. "I'm sorry, are you eating?"

"No, we're just having some mangoes. Come on over." He stood up straight as Maggie stopped at the table, then indicated Miss Evangeline with a hand.

"Maggie, this is Miss Evangeline," he said, then looked at the birdlike little woman. "And this is Maggie Redmond. She's with the Sheriff's Office."

"I know who de chile is," Miss Evangeline said, craning her neck to look up at Maggie.

"Yes, well...Maggie, our Carrie mangoes have just ripened. You need to taste this one," he said.

Before Maggie could respond, Boudreaux held out a wickedly-sharp looking knife with a perfectly orange slice of mango atop it.

"You do like mangoes, Maggie?"

"I love them, actually," she said and gingerly lifted the fruit from the blade.

"Ever' body love the mango," Miss Evangeline said.

Maggie put the fruit into her mouth and was instantly infatuated. It was completely fiberless, and the sweetest mango she could remember tasting. Her eyes shut against her will. Boudreaux saw this and smiled.

"It's really something, isn't it?"

Maggie swallowed and opened her eyes. "What's it called?"

"Carrie. It's an original Florida cultivar. Believe it or not, it's from one of the little potted trees."

He turned and pointed at one of a dozen small, potted mangoes that stood in two neat rows in front of a group of maybe twelve, full-sized trees. Boudreaux was known for cultivating mangoes in a part of Florida that was generally believed to be too far north. He had the fans, heaters, blankets and tarps to do it.

"It's amazing."

Boudreaux smiled and slid several slices onto an acrylic plate and set it in front of Miss Evangeline, who peered at it intently before turning her thick eyeglasses up to Boudreaux.

"I want some of the big one, too, me."

"The San Felipe," Boudreaux said, slicing another fruit.

"I don' need to know his name," Miss Evangeline said as she watched him cut it.

Maggie watched as Boudreaux cut the fruit from the seed in a few quick motions, then slid it onto Miss Evangeline's plate. Then Boudreaux wiped his hands on a wet towel and looked up at Maggie.

"I was just about to have a mojito. Care to join me?"

Maggie started to say she couldn't, but said "Yes" instead.

Boudreaux stepped behind a small, butcher block bar and pulled some mint leaves from a small potted plant. Miss Evangeline was eating her mango with her fingers, and had turned her attention to an open magazine, her face just a few inches from the page.

"So, Maggie," Boudreaux said, as he crushed the mint with a marble mortar and pestle. "What brings you by?"

Maggie glanced over at the old woman again before answering. "Brandon Wilmette." Boudreaux glanced up from his mint, then looked back down. "Do you know him?"

"Yes," Boudreaux said. "He's a friend of Gregory's." He pulled out two rocks glasses and divided the mint between them, then started slicing a lime. "Why are you asking about Brandon?"

"Do you know him very well?"

Boudreaux looked up and frowned at her just slightly. "Maggie, it's not like you to answer a question with a question." It felt to Maggie almost like a chastisement. "I know him well enough not to like him, but he and Gregory have been friends since college. Why do you ask?"

"That was his foot Axel Blackwell caught the other day," Maggie said.

Boudreaux stopped slicing and looked up at Maggie. "Are you sure?"

"Yes. There was a DNA sample in the system."

Boudreaux flicked the paring knife back and forth like a pencil as he frowned at her. "Is he dead, then?"

"So it would appear," Maggie answered.

"Have you found his body?"

"There might not be one."

Boudreaux glanced over at Miss Evangeline, but she seemed oblivious to them.

"Let's make our cocktails, then we'll go sit over there," Boudreaux said, pointing the knife at the other end of the porch.

He used a wooden muddler to crush the lime slices in their glasses, then grabbed some cracked ice from an ice bucket and added some to each glass. Then he poured in some simple syrup from a small decanter, added some white rum, and a little club soda. He didn't look at Maggie until he held out her glass.

"Thank you," Maggie said.

Boudreaux nodded and led her over to two white wicker chairs with blue and white striped cushions. They both sat, and each of them took a drink.

Maggie felt the need to skirt the issue for a bit. She didn't know if that was because she had questions she didn't want to ask, or questions she didn't want him to answer.

"Miss Evangeline was your housekeeper back in Louisiana?" she asked instead.

"Yes. And my nanny."

"She was the boys' nanny?" Maggie asked, meaning his two grown sons.

"Nah, she couldn't be bothered with them," Boudreaux answered. "She was just mine."

"So why is she here?"

Boudreaux looked at her. "Because I love her," he said, and took a sip of his drink.

Maggie had seen Boudreaux with his sons when they were younger, had seen him many times with his wife. But she found herself surprised to think about him loving someone, and pleased that it happened to be this tiny, raisin-like woman.

"Don't let her hatchling appearance fool you, though," Boudreaux said. "She's a voodoo-slinging velociraptor."

Maggie raised an eyebrow at him. "She practices voodoo?"

"No, not really," Boudreaux said. "But she's an advocate."

Maggie took another sip of her mojito and Bennett sighed and looked at her a moment.

"So what would you like to know about Brandon Wilmette? We called him "Sport," by the way."

"Was he at the funeral?"

"Yes. I spoke to him briefly."

"Was that the last time you saw him?"

"No. He came by my office Tuesday." Maggie waited, so he continued. "He wanted me to invest in some gourmet restaurant thing. I offered him a job instead."

"What time was that?"

"Around seven. I usually work in the evening these days."

"You didn't like him, but you offered him a job?"

"Gregory's old job. There wasn't much to it."

"Why?"

Boudreaux took another drink. "I don't like handing people money. And he'd never had an idea that he didn't screw up entirely. I didn't want to invest in his latest one."

"That sounds a lot like your description of Gregory," Maggie said, and the name was bitter on her tongue.

"They weren't all that different." He looked at her with that piercing stare he sometimes got. "Did you ever meet him?"

"No."

Hey, you want some? Maggie took another drink.

"I thought maybe you had. He spent quite a bit of time down here with Gregory."

Maggie didn't answer. "So, did he take the job?"

"He said he'd think about it. But he never got back to me."

They sat there silently for a moment, drinking their mojitos and not really looking at each other.

"It's odd, him being killed just after Gregory's funeral," Maggie said finally.

"Isn't it." he answered flatly. "So I assume you feel he's been murdered."

"Well, it's unlikely he became so despondent over Gregory that he chopped off his leg and threw himself into the sea."

Boudreaux smiled just a little. "That would be unlikely, yes."

"Although, I've been told that maybe he was gay."

Boudreaux laughed softly, obviously surprised. "Really? I wouldn't have thought that, the way he talked. But I'm not especially observant of those things."

Maggie stared at him a moment, and he met her stare. "I think you're probably very observant of everything," she said.

Boudreaux looked at her a moment and then winked.

"Unexpected 'splosive diarrhea!" cawed Miss Evangeline.

They both looked over at the old woman, who was looking in their direction triumphantly.

"Now what?" Boudreaux asked her.

"I told you them cholest'rol pill weren't no good for you, no." She poked at her magazine with one bent finger.

"Well, maybe I'll just drink your dandelion tea and choke to death instead," Boudreaux said.

Miss Evangeline stared at him blankly for a moment, running a tongue over the teeth in her upper plate.

"Go on gimme sass front o' other folk," she said quietly. "I come there an' yank you up."

Boudreaux sighed as Miss Evangeline went back to her magazine.

"If you don't need her anymore, I'll take her," Maggie said.

"She comes with her own Taser," Boudreaux said. "It was a mistake, but I can't get it back because she doesn't actually sleep."

He took a long pull of his drink and then regarded her a moment. "Is there anything else you want to know about Brandon Wilmette, Maggie?" he asked quietly.

Maggie wondered if Boudreaux knew whether Wilmette had been the other man in the woods. She wanted very much to ask, for her own sake.

"You don't seem too upset about him," she said instead.

"I'm really not." He scratched softly at an eyebrow as he looked at her "You shouldn't be, either."

Maggie was almost certain he'd just answered the question she hadn't asked. Which brought other, new questions to mind. She finished off her mojito, uncomfortable underneath his gaze.

She stood up, and Boudreaux stood with her. "Well, it's my job to figure out what happened to him," she said.

"She leavin'?" Miss Evangeline piped up.

"Yes," Maggie answered.

Miss Evangeline looked at Boudreaux and held up a plastic bag from the Piggly-Wiggly. "Put some mango in the Pilly-Willy bag for take home."

"Oh, that's all right," Maggie said, but Boudreaux was already halfway over there.

"No, you should take some," he said, as he started placing a few in the bag. "You can't get these anywhere else."

Maggie walked over to him and he held out the bag.

"Take them home to your kids," he said.

"Thank you," she said, as she took them. She looked at Miss Evangeline. "It was nice to meet you."

"You a pretty thing," Miss Evangeline said.

Maggie smiled. "Thank you. So are you."

The old woman's face scrunched up in something that might have been a smile, but could just as easily have been a heart attack.

"Goodbye, Mr. Boudreaux," Maggie said.

"It's always good to see you, Maggie," he said softly.

Maggie nodded at him, smiled again at Miss Evangeline, and headed back around to the front. Boudreaux leaned against the porch rail as he and Miss Evangeline watched her go.

"Beau'ful girl," Miss Evangeline said.

"Yes," Boudreaux said.

"Foot belong the stupid one."

"Yes."

"Juju," she said.

"Damn right," Boudreaux said quietly.

CHAPTER
EIGHT

Maggie checked her watch as she waited for the AC to assert itself in the Jeep. Then she picked up her cell and dialed Wyatt's personal phone.

"Hey," Wyatt said, cheerfully. There was a good deal of noise in the background and someone laughed loudly.

"Hey," Maggie said. "Where are you?"

"I'm at Boss Oyster," he said. "Where are you?"

"Boudreaux's driveway."

"Coming or going?"

"I'm getting ready to go home."

"How'd it go with Boudreaux?"

"It wasn't spectacularly enlightening, except that Boudreaux said he saw Wilmette on Tuesday," Maggie said, rolling down her window in an attempt to stay alive until the air kicked in. "And that he offered him a job."

"Huh. Did he take it?"

"Boudreaux says he never got back to him," Maggie said. She heard a burst of cheering in the background. "Are you watching a game?"

"Actually, I'm having a beer with your ex-husband," Wyatt said, like it was hysterical.

"You're having a beer with David?" Maggie asked. She felt a twinge of panic in her stomach, but wasn't sure why.

"Yes. In fact, we were just talking about you."

"Maybe I should come join you," Maggie said.

"That's a great idea," Wyatt said enthusiastically. "Then we can do a scene from *Seinfeld* for all the people who are already looking sideways at us."

"Why?"

"I don't know. Maybe they think it's odd, because it's odd."

"Did David ask you to come for a beer?"

"No, it was just happenstance." She heard him take a pull on his beer. "I'll see you in the morning."

"Are you sure I shouldn't come over there?"

"I'm certain of it," Wyatt said. "You have a nice night, now."

Wyatt disconnected the call, and the car suddenly seemed inordinately quiet, except for the AC. Maggie rolled up her window and backed out of the driveway.

It took a great deal of effort for her not to turn toward Boss Oyster as she headed home.

⚓ ⚓ ⚓

Wyatt closed his phone and set it back down on the bar.

"She must love this," David said, grinning.

"She seemed pretty excited about it," Wyatt said, deadpan. He drained the last of his beer and looked at David. "You want another one? On me this time."

"Sure, why not?' David answered. "I've been working on my cabin all day."

Wyatt raised his hand at the bartender and pointed at their beers. "How's that going?"

"Pretty well. It needs a lot of cosmetics, but it's a solid boat."

"I'm happy for you. I think it's great," Wyatt said. "She's proud of you."

David smiled and shrugged a bit, then looked at his empty beer bottle. "Yeah, well. The way I got the money together might not be so cool, but I'm happy, too."

Wyatt leaned a little closer to David. "How does a cop's husband manage to get into that line of work, anyway?"

David looked a little uncomfortable with the question. "She didn't tell you?"

"No. We never got into much detail on that topic."

"My cousin. He has a...uh... garden out in Tate's Hell Forest." David blinked and swallowed. "Hey, leave him alone, okay? He's small time. And he's a nice guy."

"Don't stress yourself, David," Wyatt said. "By the time I found it, it would be legal anyway."

"Well, anyway, I did some short runs for him, over to Tampa, then he vouched for me with some larger guys."

David stopped as the bartender brought them two more bottles and Wyatt handed him some cash.

Once the bartender was gone, David leaned in and spoke quietly. "I suspect it took a while for them to stop expecting Maggie to come flying in, but they were okay after a while."

Wyatt nodded. "Well, I'm glad you're out."

"Me, too," David said, nodding. He sat back and took a long swallow of his beer, then looked at Wyatt for a minute.

"What?" Wyatt finally asked him.

David shrugged and smiled. "I'm trying to come up with some way to ask your intentions without asking 'What are your intentions?'"

"Maggie," Wyatt said.

"Yeah."

Wyatt fiddled with his cork coaster a bit before answering. "They're honorable," he finally said.

David gave him a half-smile. "I was afraid of that."

"You're still in love with her."

David smiled and shook his head. "No. Sure. Of course I am." He laughed a little. "She may have thrown me out, but she never gave me a reason to not love her, man."

Wyatt nodded. David leaned his elbows on the bar.

"Listen, Wyatt. We might not hang out or play ball together anymore, but we know each other pretty well. I've always liked you. She's gonna be with somebody someday. It might as well be you."

"That's a pretty generous attitude, considering," Wyatt said.

"What else am I gonna do? She's not coming back," David said. "But she's still my best friend."

Wyatt nodded and held up his beer. David tapped it with his own and they both took a drink. Then Wyatt saw a somber look come into his eyes.

"Just don't be fooled by that tough exterior she likes to put on, man," David said. "She's more vulnerable than she lets on."

"Okay."

David picked at the label on his bottle for a bit. "She gets these nightmares, always has. Some old lady chasing her down a beach. She won't talk about them, so don't ask. But it helps if you're just there."

"I'm not sleeping with your ex-wife, David," Wyatt said gently.

David looked over at him and smiled. "I'm all kinds of happy to hear that," he said. "But you will be."

"How do you know?"

"Because your intentions are honorable," David said with a shrug. He took a swallow of his beer before speaking again. "I don't know if she's ever told you, but she's never been with anyone but me."

"She's told me."

"She's not the sleeping around type. She's been married pretty much her whole life and that's what type she is."

"If it makes you feel any better, that's part of her appeal," Wyatt said.

"Good." David smiled and shook his head. "Like I said, it might as well be you."

He and Wyatt each took another drink, and David sat back and looked at Wyatt more seriously. "But, man, I'll tell you what. You hurt her, and I swear I'll beat your ass."

Wyatt remembered Gray Redmond saying almost that very thing to him the night Maggie had taken him over for dinner. He nodded. "I get that a lot lately."

⚓ ⚓ ⚓

When Maggie pulled up in front of her house, Kyle was feeding the chickens, and Sky was sitting at the bottom of the stairs, earbuds in, texting someone on her phone.

Stoopid made a wings-akimbo beeline for the car from some mysterious location, but was run over by Coco halfway there. Once he righted himself, he proceeded onward and gave Maggie one of his odd, broken crows before heading over to see what Kyle was dispensing.

Coco fragmented at Maggie's feet, and she bent down and gave Coco's tummy a rub. When she stood up, Sky had pulled one earbud out.

"Hey," Sky said.

"Hey. How was your day?"

"Dude. Sucked like a Dyson," Sky said. "Bella got dumped by her boyfriend and I've spent like the whole day keeping her head out of the oven."

Maggie stopped at the bottom of the stairs. "Well, he was probably a dink, anyway, but tell her I'm sorry."

"She'll get over it, but you know how she is. Right now, the world is commencing to end," Sky said. "But we want to know if we can just stay here tomorrow night."

"You don't want to go to 3rd of July?"

"Not really. I mean, it's cool and all, but we're going out to the island for the 4th, anyway. We're just gonna rent some movies and I'm gonna redo her highlights. Highlights fix everything."

Kyle piped up from behind Maggie.

"If Sky's having a sleepover, can I stay home?"

Maggie turned and ran a hand through his hair. "Don't you want to go?"

"Nah. I'd rather hang out at home. It's too crowded over there."

"Well, it's up to your sister." Maggie looked at Sky, but she already had her earbud back in.

Maggie pointed, and Sky pulled it out. "What?" she asked.

"Kyle wants to stay home tomorrow. I told him it's up to you."

"I don't care, as long as he doesn't mind helping us wax our armpits."

"What?" Kyle asked, looking mildly alarmed.

"It's a joke, dork."

She stood up as Kyle headed up the stairs, then she stuck a finger in his ear as he passed. He laughed and brushed it away.

"What about your Dad, though?' Maggie asked. "He's probably looking forward to seeing you there."

"No, we were texting earlier," Sky said. "He might go, but only for a little while and he's not staying for the fireworks. He's working tomorrow night so he can go the island with us."

"Well, I guess I'll have to hang out with Grandma and Granddad, then," Maggie said as she followed Sky up the stairs.

"It'll be way cooler," Sky said. "You can act weird without us seeing you."

"Geez, you're such a jerk," Maggie laughed.

She followed Sky into the house, where Kyle was already entrenched on the couch with Minecraft.

"Hang out with Wyatt," Sky said, heading for the hallway and her room.

"I'm not allowed to hang out with Wyatt," Maggie said.

"Well, then quit it."

⚓ ⚓ ⚓

Later that night, Maggie luxuriated in a long shower, pulled on some yoga pants, and she and Coco went through the sliding door in the living room to sit outside to sit on the back deck. Sky was plugged into Netflix in her room, and Kyle had already gone to bed, though it was just getting dark.

Maggie stood at the railing and peeled the one mango that was left after she and the kids had torn into them. She threw the peels down to Stoopid, who was pulling sentry duty on an overturned rowboat in the back yard, then leaned over the railing as she tried to eat the mango without having to change clothes.

As she did, she thought about Wilmette and Gregory Boudreaux. Wilmette didn't come to town until after Gregory was dead, but he did get here before that letter from Gregory was mailed. Did he send it? If he did, why? Did he feel bad about watching while Gregory raped a fifteen-year old girl?

Then there was Boudreaux. Maggie's feelings about Boudreaux became more conflicted every time they spoke. He hadn't crossed her path more than five times in her life before Gregory's death. She'd only thought of him in distant terms, and those were all focused on his supposed involvement in everything from interfering with unions to buying politicians.

There had been rumors, through the years, that he'd been involved in more than one missing person or sudden change of heart from a potential witness. It was also suspected that he might be in the drug trade, but he'd never even been indicted of anything. That could have as much to do with his son Patrick being the assistant State's Attorney as it did with him being innocent, but innocence was unlikely.

Yet, Maggie found herself drawn to him. He was compelling and he was oddly frank with her at times. She also found him funny and actually quite interesting. It was more than that, she knew, but she couldn't put her finger on it in a way that satisfied her. There was a decent chance he meant her some kind of harm, and yet she found herself comfortable in his presence.

Boudreaux knew Gregory had raped Maggie. He'd hinted it carefully enough when she was investigating Gregory's death. She felt that he had also told her, without telling her, that Wilmette had been the other man in the woods that day. But, why? Did he think that gave him some kind of leverage over her? She'd always been pretty sure that he suspected she'd shot Gregory and made it look like suicide. Did he think she'd killed Wilmette, too?

She discarded that last thought pretty quickly. Her instincts told her he knew she didn't. They hinted that he knew that because *he* had killed Wilmette, but that just created more questions, chiefly why? Wilmette wanted money. Had he been blackmailing Gregory or Boudreaux or both?

Maggie threw the mango pit out to the river and sighed in frustration.

Too many questions. Not a single answer that appealed to her at all.

CHAPTER

NINE

T he next day dawned sultry and thick, and promised
misery to those who despised heat. Maggie got to Riverfront Park, at the end of Water Street downtown,
just after 5:00 p.m., and the heat was still oppressive.
The 3rd of July, as it was still being called in its fourth
year, had become a huge event for the town. Saint George
Island had a big Independence Day event that many of the
locals attended, but some of the town leaders and business
owners had decided to create their own, a day early, so
that folks could enjoy an event there in town, without having to miss other happenings on the 4th.

Maggie found a place to park a few blocks away, and
headed to the park. The street in front of the park was
blocked off to traffic for the day, and filled with almost
shoulder-to-shoulder people enjoying a bluegrass band.
The aromas of fish fingers, burgers and firecracker shrimp
assaulted Maggie, as she threaded her way through the
crowd. Wyatt was working the event during the afternoon,
but Maggie was supposed to meet her parents at the far end
of the park, near the seawall.

She grabbed a bottled water and a sweet tea from one of the vendors, and finally located her folks, parked in stadium chairs with little tables and cup holders built into them. Maggie saw there was an extra one for her.

"Hey, y'all," Maggie said, and bent to kiss the top of her father's head.

"Hey, Sunshine," her dad said with a big smile.

Maggie hugged her mom, then plopped down in the empty chair beside her. "Man, this crowd is getting bigger every year," she said.

"I know it is," Georgia said. "It was already packed when we got here."

"Hey, Maggie!"

Maggie looked over her shoulder to see John Solomon approaching, wearing a huge smile and a stained white apron.

John was the director of the Chamber of Commerce, but he'd spent twenty years with the Sheriff's Office as the head of IT, until he'd taken his retirement. He was a great guy, and Maggie missed having him around, but he'd found his calling.

"Hey, John," Maggie said. "Looks like you have a lot of burgers to cook."

"Oh, man, Maggie," he said, laughing. "I've been at that grill since ten o'clock."

"You're in your element," Gray said. "I don't envy you working a grill in this heat, though."

"Ah, it's starting to cool down a bit," John said. "There's a chance I might not die."

⚓ ⚓ ⚓

A couple of hours later, David had joined Maggie and her parents with an old deck chair, and had a couple of beers as they listened to the music and watched everyone jockey for patches of grass, blanket and seawall so they could watch the fireworks. Dusk had come, a breeze had arrived, and anticipation was high.

Maggie's butt hurt from sitting so long, and she was about to get up and stretch her legs when Wyatt showed up beside her chair.

"Hey, guys," he said.

Everyone said hello back and Maggie stuck her now unnecessary sunglasses on top of her head, as Wyatt squatted down next to her, a plastic cup of beer in his hand.

"Where are your kids?" he asked her.

"They bailed. They're at the house," she said.

Wyatt nodded.

"You finally off duty?" Gray asked.

"Yep, as of right now," Wyatt said, and took off his cap to run a hand through his hair.

"Well, I've got to go *on* duty," David said, looking at his cell phone. "Mike and his cousin are ready to shove off."

"You going out tonight, David?" Wyatt asked.

"Yeah," David said, and grinned. "Gonna be a heck of a show from out on the water."

He stood up, then shook Gray's hand. "See you, later, Gray."

"Keep the hull down," Gray said.

"Take care, David," Georgia said.

"I will, Ma," he answered.

He shook Wyatt's hand, then turned to bend down to Maggie, but she stood up and stretched her back, then gave him a hug.

"See you later, babe," he said.

"See you later," she told him, then let him go. As he started off, she grabbed his hand. "Hey!"

He stopped and looked at her.

"Break those nets," she said.

"You know it," he said, then gave her a wink and walked away.

A few minutes later, Maggie looked down at Wyatt. "I need to stretch my legs. Wanna come?"

"Yep," he said, and stood up.

"We'll be back, you guys," Maggie said, and Wyatt followed her as she walked over toward the far end of the seawall.

She stopped at the concrete drive that divided the park from the house next to it, leaned a hip on one of the wood pilings that lined the park, just a few feet from the seawall. Across the river, she could see lots of activity on the fireworks barge, as the crew got ready for the show. It would be dark in twenty minutes or so, and she could see people hurrying back and forth on the deck.

She looked up at Wyatt, who was taking a drink of his beer. "So, how was your night?"

"You mean how was my night with David?" Wyatt asked, trying not to grin.

"Yeah."

"It was nice. We're thinking about seeing each other again." He waggled his eyebrows at her. "Would that be really awkward, me dating your ex-husband?"

Maggie smiled. "Why are you such a jerk?"

"Because it gets you all twitterpated, and I think you're just precious when you're twitterpated."

"Seriously. What did you guys talk about?"

Wyatt took another sip of his beer, and watched as a shrimp boat headed their way from the docks up river. "The Bucs, bless their little hearts. Shrimp. Boxers versus briefs. There was a little bit about you in there, too."

"Wyatt."

"You're a good woman. We agreed on that. I'm a good guy. We agreed on that, too. If I hurt you, he'll climb up my legs and beat my ass. There was some disagreement, there, but nothing we can't work through."

Maggie felt a warmth creep into her chest. David, her lifetime protector, even now, even with Wyatt.

The first time she'd really noticed him, when they were ten years old, he was pulling Regina Sparks off of Maggie's back, as she spit sand out of her mouth and struggled for air. As Maggie recalled, Regina had felt that Maggie had busted her in the nose with the tetherball on purpose.

Maybe she had; she couldn't remember. But, Regina had been yanked off of her and a hand had been held out, and Maggie had been helped to her feet by a boy with hair like black diamonds and a skateboard under his arm.

"Well, make no mistake," said Maggie with a smile. "He'll do it. So mind your P's and Q's."

"You have nothing to fear from any part of my alphabet."

Wyatt winked at her, and she turned around to look at the river. David's pretty old blue Jefferson was just passing by. Mike, the huge black man who crewed for Axel, was at the helm. A much smaller, much thinner black man was leaning against the port side, drinking what would probably be the first of many cups of coffee. David was on the starboard side, facing the park, one hand hanging onto one of the ropes that held his nets.

Maggie smiled as he passed, feeling self-conscious about the fact that Wyatt was standing next to her, but David smiled back. She waved at him, and he held up a hand in response, as a muffled *boom* sounded.

Maggie wondered why the fireworks were starting already, then there was another *thump*, and David was gone, swallowed by an enormous ball of fire.

CHAPTER TEN

For two eternal seconds, Maggie's brain stopped processing information from her ears and eyes, stopped sending commands to her body. Then everything came back at once. Chaos erupted around her, and she kicked off her deck shoes and took one running step toward the seawall before a large hand grabbed the leather belt threaded through her shorts.

"No, dammit!" Wyatt yelled. She spun around. "The river's on fire, Maggie! Come on."

He grabbed her hand, and she ran after him, shoeless but not noticing, as he pushed and yelled his way through the people that were flocking to the seawall, and the people who were running away from it.

In the corner of her eye, Maggie saw Deputy Dwight Shultz, in uniform, running toward them.

"Sheriff!" he yelled.

Wyatt didn't slow down. "You call Fire?" he yelled back.

"Yes sir—" he started, but they had already run out of hearing range over the pandemonium in the park.

Maggie sort of noticed that there were men running in front of and behind them, all of them oystermen or shrimpers, all of them heading for the docks, but the fact registered only in the vaguest terms.

She also vaguely understood that she was barefoot, and that rocks, bits of oyster shell and other objects were cutting her feet as she ran. But, her only real, solid thought was that she shouldn't be running *away* from David.

They reached the dock at Scipio where they tied up the powerboat used by the Sheriff's office, the one Maggie had docked just the other day, when the worst thing happening was a severed leg in a net.

Maggie heard feet pounding behind and around her, as men ran for other boats and other docks. She and Wyatt reached the 90s-era Wellcraft that belonged to the SO courtesy of a coke bust, and Maggie bent down to hurriedly untie the stern line. She heard running footsteps stop behind her.

"Are you crazy?" Boudreaux asked, raising his voice. She stood and spun around. "You can't take that outboard out there."

Maggie thought, oddly, how surprised she was to see Boudreaux. He usually didn't attend July 3rd.

He looked up at Wyatt. "Come on," he said, as he spun around.

They ran after him, toward a couple of shrimp boats on the next dock. He leased the boats out to some of the locals, then bought the shrimp they brought in on them.

A big, bearded man whose name Maggie couldn't remember was already firing up the engine, and two other guys were getting the stern and bow lines. There were men in the boat across the dock, doing the same. Boudreaux jumped nimbly onto the starboard side, jumped down onto the deck, and turned to grab Maggie's hand. She took it and jumped down to the deck, then Wyatt followed.

"You have the fire department on the way?" Boudreaux asked.

"Yes," Wyatt said.

"Maggie! I'm coming, too!"

Maggie turned toward the dock and saw her father standing there, his chest heaving. Georgia was a few steps behind him, her face streaked with tears.

"No, Daddy!" Maggie yelled, feeling panic threaten to assert itself in her stomach. "You can't get near that smoke!"

Gray had been diagnosed with Stage 1 lung cancer a little over a year earlier, although he'd never smoked. He'd been fortunate, but he'd lost part of his left lung.

"Mom, keep him away from the smoke," Maggie yelled, and then they were underway.

"Todd, turn that spotlight on," Boudreaux called to the bearded man, and the man reached over and turned on the spotlight on the front of the small, aft cabin. "Sheriff, there's another one on the bow."

Wyatt grabbed Maggie's shoulder and looked at her face. "You okay?"

Maggie nodded, and he ran toward the bow as they motored toward the flames. Maggie ran to the starboard rail. Docked boats were still blocking a good view of David's boat, but the sky was lighter, tinged with orange and blue and white, just above the old Jefferson. The boat itself was engulfed, from the aft cabin to the stern.

How many minutes ago had David hugged her goodbye? Three? Five? Ten? Maggie got a sensory memory of warm cotton, Jovan musk, and Suave shampoo, and something large and hard and threatening almost closed her throat.

Once the shrimp boat cleared the marina and came into the river in front of the park, the smell of diesel and smoke were overwhelming. The other shrimp boat belonging to Boudreaux was ahead of them, and started to angle toward the park side of the wreckage, while their boat headed around the other way.

It was full-on dark now, and the fire, spotlights, and dozens of flashlights from the seawall reflected on the black water. Here and there, burning pieces of debris floated on the surface. The portside outrigger had collapsed against the side, and its net spread out on the water like a broken wing.

Maggie leaned over the starboard rail as they got closer, and the bearded man cut back the engine just a bit. "David!" she called.

The center and stern deck were almost completely gone, and Maggie knew that David was in the water. She strained to make sense of the various dark shapes that littered the surface, but tore her eyes from the water when she saw that they were going past the Jefferson.

"What are you doing?" she yelled at Boudreaux, who was at the starboard rail as well, further aft.

"Maggie, they're gonna get carried that way," he yelled back, bending and straightening his arm to indicate the mouth of the bay. "We're gonna circle back."

Maggie turned back to the water and leaned further over the rail, as though this would help her see better. Suddenly, she heard a commotion of voices from the seawall at the park, and she saw John Solomon, recognizable by the white apron, as he stepped off the seawall into the river, a life preserver from who knew where in one hand, a rope in the other. Another man stood at the seawall holding the other end of the rope. Maggie stopped breathing, as she watched John grab something that was lodged against one of the old dock pilings. As he threw it onto his shoulder, Maggie saw that it was a very large, very black arm.

The other shrimp boat angled over toward John at a crawl, as he pulled Mike's arm through the life preserver, then brought it down over his head.

Maggie turned her attention back to the water's surface. She could hear the firetrucks approaching from downtown, and she knew the Coast Guard and the fire boats would be there any minute to subdue the fire, but David wasn't on his brand-new old boat that he'd saved for, and Maggie didn't care about the fire. David was in the water.

About forty yards past the Jefferson, she felt the trawler slow and begin to turn to starboard and go back up river. Boudreaux and the other man ran to the port side to examine the surface, while Maggie stayed starboard.

A few moments later, she saw it. An arm, a mostly white one, lying on a piece of the hull. She traced it, saw the back of David's green plaid flannel shirt. "There's David," she yelled, and had climbed up and dived off the rail before Boudreaux and the other man had turned around.

"Todd!" Boudreaux yelled, and when the bearded man turned around, Boudreaux pointed over in the direction in which Maggie was furiously swimming. Todd nodded and turned to starboard.

Wyatt came flying back from the bow. "Dammit, dammit, *dammit!*" he yelled as he ran.

He met Boudreaux and the other man as they arrived at the starboard rail. Boudreaux opened one of the built-in boxes and pulled out a bright red rescue tube like lifeguards carried, a rope already tied at one end. He deftly tied the other end to the rail, never taking his eyes off the water.

Wyatt pulled a large, industrial flashlight out of the box and turned it on, pointed it at Maggie's head as she approached the hunk of shattered wood.

Maggie took a deep breath and powered through the last few yards, struggling to swim across and up the current. She finally reached David, and grabbed onto the hull with her right hand. The back of David's shirt was almost burned away, and the back of his head was bleeding and burned and missing some hair.

She grabbed the back of his collar with her left hand, and pulled him backward onto her chest. He started to slide downward, and she got her left arm underneath his, wrapped it around his chest, and cried out as she dragged him back up her body. Then she leaned backwards in the water, as far as she could without letting go of the piece of hull.

"I've got you, baby," she gasped. "I've got you."

David's head lolled on her left shoulder, his face buried in her neck. She pressed her face against his as she struggled to keep her arm under his, and her grip on the jagged edge of the hull.

"It's okay," she whispered. "It's okay."

The trawler lumbered alongside a moment later, its small wake pushing Maggie and David up against the hull, even as it pushed the hull further away. She loosened her grip on the broken wood long enough to get a better purchase on it.

The light from Wyatt's flashlight blinded her suddenly as it shone in her face, and then the rescue tube slapped down in the water beside her. She let go of the hull, and she and David both went underwater a second, until she reached across their bodies and grabbed hold of the tube. She felt a sharp tug, and they were dragged toward the trawler.

As she came out of the focus of the flashlight, she saw the silhouette of Boudreaux as he pulled her in. Then she saw Wyatt pass the flashlight to Boudreaux's man and then lean over the rail.

Maggie let go of the rope just long enough to grab it closer to the rescue tube itself, then wrap her arm around it a few loops to give her some buoyancy. Wyatt was leaning as far as possible over the rail, but even with his height, his hand was still too far away to grab hold of David anywhere.

Maggie let go of David's chest just long enough to grab his left bicep instead and lift his arm.

"I got him," Wyatt barked, as he grabbed David's hand. He pulled David off of her, and pulled him out of the water up to his waist. Boudreaux leaned over the rail and grabbed David's other arm. His crewman had a hand looped into the back of Boudreaux's belt to steady him.

"Be careful of his back," Maggie yelled, as they got David to the rail, then Boudreaux let go of his arm and grabbed his feet.

They carefully lifted David over the rail and laid him down, then Wyatt leaned over and stuck out his hand. Maggie reached up and grabbed it, and he hauled her over. She fell down to her knees next to David. Given the state of his back, his face looked surprisingly normal, but for the watery blood that dribbled from his nose and right ear.

As the engine revved and the boat sped up, Maggie put a hand on David's chest. He wasn't breathing. She pinched his nose shut, took a breath, and clamped her mouth down onto his. She felt his chest rise just slightly as she pushed the air into him. She did it again, only vaguely hearing Wyatt speaking. She took her mouth away one more time, started to take a breath.

"Maggie," Wyatt said quietly, kneeling down on the other side of David. "Stop."

"He's been underwater, Wyatt!"

"It's not the water," he said, and laid a hand on top of hers, where it rested atop David's motionless chest. She jerked her hand away, just as she felt a hand under her other arm and Boudreaux gently, but firmly, pulled her to her feet.

"He's dead, Maggie," Boudreaux said quietly.

Maggie pulled her right arm back and punched him in the face.

CHAPTER
ELEVEN

When the trawler pulled back in to the dock, a handful of paramedics and Maggie's parents were waiting there, though Maggie didn't really see them.

She sat on the deck, up against the side. David's body leaned back against her, his head on her chest, and she had her arms wrapped loosely around him.

"My babies," Georgia said, and covered her mouth as she burst into tears.

Boudreaux's man threw the line to Gray, who tied it off before jumping down into the boat. Gray nodded at Wyatt, who was standing at the rail next to Maggie, cap in hand. Then he looked at Boudreaux, who was standing a few feet away. Boudreaux nodded, then Gray knelt down in front of Maggie.

He put a hand on either side of her face, but Maggie didn't look at him.

"Maggie," he said quietly. "Give him to me."

Maggie didn't move, and Gray put his hands under David's underarms.

"Stop it, Daddy," Maggie said quietly.

"Give him to me, sweetie," he said more firmly, and pulled David to him, leaned him against his chest. Maggie reached out and grabbed a piece of David's black and shredded shirt.

Two paramedics jumped down into the boat. They knelt down next to Gray, and Maggie had to let go of David's shirt as Gray gently laid him down on the deck. The paramedics bent over David as Wyatt leaned down and put his hands under Maggie's arms and lifted her to her feet.

Two more paramedics came aboard with a gurney. Maggie gently pushed Wyatt away, and stood and watched as the first two responders gently lifted David to the gurney.

David's left arm slipped off, and as the paramedic carefully put it back on the stretcher, Maggie noticed for the first time the white strip of skin around his ring finger. At some point recently, he had finally removed his wedding band. It had taken more than five years.

That, finally, finished the breaking of her heart. Tears sprang to her eyes, but she blinked them back. Something loud and primal wanted to come out of her throat, so she clamped her lips shut. She could hear her mom crying quietly on the dock, and thought that she should go and comfort her, but she just couldn't.

Gray put a hand on her shoulder as one of the paramedics, Boyd Watson, stepped forward. "I'm so sorry, Maggie."

Maggie didn't look at him, just watched as David's body was strapped down to the gurney. There was a smear of blood next to his head, as large as the palm of a hand. She hadn't noticed David was bleeding much, and she looked down at her yellow tee shirt. It was covered in blood.

She began to shake, and Boyd looked at Wyatt. "Maybe I should give her something," he said.

Maggie waved him away, slipped out from under her father's hand, and walked across the deck.

"Leave her alone," Wyatt said quietly, and followed Maggie as she stepped up onto the dock.

Boudreaux's eyes were flat as he watched them go, absentmindedly rubbing the left side of his jaw.

⚓ ⚓ ⚓

Maggie's parents had driven her home. Georgia drove Maggie's Jeep, and Maggie rode with Gray in his truck. Not a word was spoken on the way to the house. Once they got there, Maggie ignored Coco and Stoopid, leaned on Gray's truck and steeled herself to go inside to her children.

She was incredibly grateful when her dad handed her his navy windbreaker. She had forgotten about the blood. She slipped it on and zipped it all the way to the neck.

A few minutes later, they went inside, and Georgia took Bella outside and sat with her on the steps to wait for her mom, while Maggie and Gray broke the news to Sky and Kyle. Kyle was alarmingly calm and quiet, but he crawled onto Maggie's lap on the couch. Sky screamed, then cried on her mother's shoulder, then was held for a long while by her granddad. When she came back inside, Georgia made hot tea and then looked around the kitchen for some other way to minister to Maggie and the children.

After a while, Maggie took a shower and slipped on some yoga pants. She tied her bloody clothes up in a Piggly-Wiggly bag and put it in the back of her closet. Then she went back out to the living room to be with her family.

Throughout this time, Maggie hadn't shed a tear, though a torrent of them threatened continuously. She felt she needed to wait for some better time, some private time, when her kids needed just a little bit less for her to be strong.

Eventually, Sky stopped crying and curled up silently on Gray's chest, next to Maggie and Kyle. Georgia could find no more to do, and settled into one of the armchairs across from the couch.

It was past midnight when Maggie realized how much her thighs hurt. Kyle was sound asleep in her lap, and she gently laid him down on one of the sofa pillows. His black bangs fell over one impossibly long-lashed eye. So much like David's. Maggie saw David, eyes closed, lying on the deck, and pieces of her fell into the ocean.

She pulled her right knee up to her chest to flex the muscle, and Georgia gasped. "Oh honey, your feet."

Relieved to find some way she could be useful, Georgia hurried down the hall to get the first aid kit Maggie kept in the linen closet. Maggie flexed her other leg and looked over at Sky. She was just inches away, but she hadn't spoken to Maggie since her first few, unbelieving questions. She had spoken only to Gray. Now, she stared at an empty spot in the middle of the room.

Maggie reached over and put a hand on her daughter's, where it rested on Gray's thigh.

"Sky, baby," she said. Sky pulled her hand away slowly, curled it against her chest. "Sky, do you want some of your water?"

Sky finally turned her eyes to her mother's face. "No," she said flatly.

Maggie reached up to Sky's face, intending to touch her cheek, but Sky suddenly reached up and slapped it away. "Leave me alone!" she snapped, then jumped up from the couch.

"Sky—" Gray started.

"He only bought that boat because of you!" Sky spat at Maggie, then hurried past Georgia as she came back into the room. They heard Sky's door slam down the hall.

Maggie swallowed hard, then looked at Gray. "Help me, Daddy," she said softly.

Gray put his arm around Maggie's neck and pulled her to him, buried his face in her hair and kissed her head. It almost broke her, and she straightened up, as Georgia sat down on the coffee table and picked up one of Maggie's feet.

"Oh, my Lord," Georgia said.

Maggie reached down with her right hand and gently took her mother's hand away as she retracted her foot. Georgia snatched at her hand and turned it palm up. "Look at your hand!"

There was one fairly deep, jagged slice across Maggie's palm, surrounded by several small scratches, from the splintered wood of David's shattered hull. Georgia held onto Maggie's hand as she flipped open the first aid kit.

"No, Mom," Maggie said quietly, pulling her hand back.

Georgia grabbed the hand back and looked kindly, but firmly, at her daughter. "Will you be more useful to your children with a raging infection, Margaret Anne?"

Maggie looked away and swallowed, but she didn't take her hand back. It didn't seem right for her to have such minor wounds attended to. It didn't seem fair for her to have wounds that would heal.

Georgia had cleaned, treated, and wrapped a strip of gauze around Maggie's palm, and had just finished applying antibiotic cream to Maggie's feet when Kyle stirred, then sat up.

"Mom," he said, only half awake.

Maggie stood up and took his hand. "C'mon, buddy. Let's get you to bed."

Kyle stood, swaying just a bit, then Maggie followed him into the hall. He turned left instead of right, pulled back the covers, and crawled into Maggie's bed, on the far side. He was still wearing his cargo shorts and a Third Day tee shirt. Maggie pulled the covers up over him, then went back out to the hall. Gray and Georgia were right there, heading for Kyle's room.

"We're going to sleep in Kyle's room," Gray said quietly. "You need to try to get some rest."

"Wake us up if you need anything," Georgia said.

Maggie nodded, then turned and went back into her room.

She crawled under the covers with Kyle, who was already asleep again. She reached out and ran her fingers through his bangs, but his likeness to his father, as he laid on David's old side of the bed, was more than she could handle. She turned toward the door, and Coco jumped up, settled at the end of the bed, and rested her chin on Maggie's feet with a sigh.

A few hours later, Maggie still hadn't slept. Sky appeared in her doorway without a sound. Maggie strained to see her face in the dark.

"I didn't mean it," Sky finally said, and there was a trembling in her voice. "I don't know why I said that."

Maggie pulled the covers down, and Sky crawled in beside her, curled her back into Maggie. Maggie put her arm around her and breathed deeply.

Sky fell asleep within a few minutes, but Maggie never did. She blinked several thousand times, but never closed her eyes, and never shed a tear.

Ever since the rape, Maggie had been able to compartmentalize feelings that were just too much for her to handle. She could push them down, push them back, make them wait for another time.

Intellectually, she knew that it was considered unhealthy, a symptom of damage. She considered it a bonus, some kind of recompense for the occasional nightmares and flashbacks, this ability to protect herself. She refused to call it PTSD, to give Gregory Boudreaux anything more than he had already taken. And right now, she was as grateful for it as she could imagine being.

⚓ ⚓ ⚓

When the sky finally began to lighten outside Maggie's bedroom window, she carefully climbed out of bed and went to the bathroom. She could hear her father snoring faintly through Kyle's open door.

After using the restroom, Maggie went to the kitchen and made a pot of coffee, more out of habit than anything else. Although she hadn't slept, she didn't feel the lack of it. Once her coffee was made, she grabbed it and her cell phone and went outside.

Coco ran off to do her business in the trees, and Stoopid pell-melled across the gravel to announce that he had spotted Maggie, or that it was daytime, or that the sky had fallen. Maggie sidestepped him, gave him a rote "Morning, Stoopid," then went and fed the girls. After the chickens had been fed, Coco followed Maggie up to the deck, and Maggie sat down to check her cell phone, again, purely out of habit.

She'd missed two calls from Wyatt, but couldn't bring herself to listen to his voice mails. He'd called and talked to Gray last night, asked after their wellbeing, but Maggie hadn't been able to talk to him. The man she'd loved her whole life was lying in the morgue at Weems Memorial. She just couldn't make herself talk to the man she'd probably end up loving next.

TWELVE

Maggie spent the rest of the day going through the paperwork that she and David shared on wills, wishes and insurance. She talked to the insurance company about making arrangements for David's cremation, as per his wishes, declined to answer her cell phone, and politely refused to speak to those people who decided to try one of her parents instead.

She also hugged her children a great deal, called the fire department three times to see if they had any news on the cause of the explosion, and was left with nothing other than that they were working diligently. She knew little about fire or explosions, but she did know a bit more about boats, and she and her father sat on the deck and discussed possibilities at length. The trawler carried a lot of diesel, but diesel was slow to ignite. Propane was much more sensitive, but David only had a large enough tank down below to fuel the galley.

Neither of them could recall if they'd seen any fireworks after that first, muffled *whump*. That moment inserted itself into Maggie's mind hundreds of times that day, and she tried to make herself notice the sky in retrospect. But all she saw was David's smile, and his wave, and she could think was *Jump!* No matter how many times she remembered it, he never did.

Late in the afternoon, Gray came out into the little dining area near the front door, where Maggie sat with an uneaten sandwich and a cold cup of tea. Georgia was in Sky's room, helping the kids fold some laundry she'd found to do. Maggie looked up as Gray sat down across the cypress table his father had built.

"Sweetheart, the kids want to come back to the house with us," he said quietly. "There's just too much of David here right now. But they don't want to leave you here."

"I know I should go with them, Daddy," she said. "It's not fair to ask them to stay, and it's selfish to be away from them. I'm just so afraid that I'm finally going to come apart, and I can't stand for them to see it."

Gray nodded. "Why don't you call Wyatt, Maggie?"

Maggie shook her head. "No." She blinked back a sudden heat in her eyes. "Being with Wyatt didn't feel like cheating before, but it does now."

Gray took a deep breath, then sighed and grabbed both of her hands up in his.

"Let me tell you something you're not ready to believe right now," he said. "But I want you to remember it for when you are ready to believe it. David loved you and he wanted you to be happy. If that meant you being with Wyatt, well, he might not have liked it, but he wanted it for you. You do him a disservice if you ignore that."

Maggie blinked again and looked away, out the living room window.

"I know you're in pain, Maggie," he said firmly. "But I know you hear me, too."

He stood up, then came around and placed a hand on her shoulder, kissed the top of her head. She squeezed his hand.

"We'll get some things together for the kids," Gray said. "Your Mama left a pot of soup on the stove for you."

A short time after her parents and children left, Wyatt called Maggie's phone for the third time in an hour. She felt horrible for ignoring it, but she did anyway. A moment later, he texted her.

Pulling in with David's truck.

Her chest tightened as she set down the phone, and she had just slipped into her flip-flops by the door when Coco started whining and leaping. By the time she got the door open, Maggie could hear the familiar, slightly hollow hum of David's old Toyota pickup.

Coco nearly fell down the deck stairs as the truck pulled into the parking area in front of the house, a Sheriff's cruiser behind it.

"Coco!" Maggie called, thinking she could warn her poor dog somehow, but Coco was beyond hearing. Stoopid flew out from under the house, but Coco's excitement was too much for his nerves, so he veered off into the flower garden.

Maggie was at the bottom of the stairs when Wyatt opened the door. It took a second for Coco to process that the wrong man had climbed from the truck, but she liked Wyatt, and tried to look happy, even though her body wagged much more slowly.

Wyatt reached down and rubbed Coco's head, then walked around to the front of the truck, where Maggie stood.

"I'm sorry. I know you don't want to talk to anybody right now. Or me." Wyatt put his hands on his hips. "But I couldn't just pull up in David's truck without warning you."

Maggie swallowed hard and nodded. She found it hard to look him in the eye. On the one hand, she wanted to run to him. On the other, she wanted to insist that he shouldn't be here, where she and David had conceived their children.

She peered around the truck and saw Dwight at the wheel of the idling cruiser. She finally looked up at Wyatt. "I keep calling the fire department, but they keep telling me they don't have any news. Do you know what happened yet?"

Wyatt looked down at Coco, who was sitting at Maggie's feet.

"Not yet," he answered. He took off his hat and ran a hand through his hair, the way he did, then he looked at her. "Do you want me to stay for a while? I can get a ride back later."

She was going to just say no, but he looked so concerned, she felt he at least deserved some honesty. "I do, but I don't," she said, and tried not to let it be hurtful. "I just need to be alone for a bit."

He nodded, looked beyond her at the yard for a minute before looking her in the eye. "You know that I care. And you know where I am. When you need me," he added.

Maggie nodded and wrapped her arms around herself, like she could hold herself back from just walking into his chest and hiding there. He looked at her for another moment, then put his hat back on and walked to the cruiser and got in.

Maggie watched them go, then stood and stared at the truck that David had bought while they were still married. She slowly, almost fearfully, walked to the driver's side and looked through the open window. A photo keychain hung from the rear view mirror, the kids in it three years younger.

She jumped when she heard a trilling, then reached into her back pocket and answered the phone.

"Hello?"

"Maggie, it's Larry," said the old medical examiner.

Maggie swallowed hard. "Hello, Larry."

"I wanted you to know, because I know you," he started. "David died from severe concussive trauma to the brain. There was no water in his lungs. I hoped that this would bring you some comfort."

Maggie closed her eyes.

"You couldn't have saved him, even if you'd found him as soon as he hit the water. Do you understand?"

"Yes," Maggie said, and didn't recognize the small voice. "Thank you."

"I'm so very sorry, my friend. I truly am."

Maggie blinked several times before speaking. "Do you know when—when he'll be released?"

"I have most of what I need. Whatever arrangements you've made, he can be picked up as early as tomorrow afternoon."

"Thank you. Larry."

She hung up the phone and closed her eyes again. Coco jumped up and laid her paws on the door, could just get her snout to the window. Maggie saw her nose twitch, and she knew Coco picked up much more than she did; which was the faint scent of Jovan musk.

Maggie's chest clenched, and she turned away from the window, slid down the door and sat in the dirt. Coco dropped to all fours and whined, nuzzled Maggie's hand. Maggie put her arms around the dog's shoulders and buried her face in Coco's neck.

"Oh, Coco," she said into her fur. "Daddy went away."

THIRTEEN

L ess than an hour later, Wyatt's cruiser pulled into the driveway next to David's truck.

Maggie was sitting on the deck. Beside her was David's old guitar, the one he'd given to Sky and Kyle when Maggie had bought him a new one a few years back. Maggie had dragged it out of the corner of the living room and held it on her lap for a long time. She had heard *Waterbound* playing from it, heard David's soft voice singing the words, as he had hundreds of times, at her request. It had always been her favorite. She'd heard it in her head, and wished that she had recorded him just once. She was suddenly afraid that she would forget how it had sounded.

Coco barreled down the stairs, and Maggie walked to the front deck. She watched Wyatt get out and walk to the bottom of the stairs.

"I'm sorry. I lied to you," he said.

"About what?"

"Can I come up?"

"Yes," she said, and she noticed that her hands were trembling on the rail. "Do you want some coffee?" she asked when he got there.

"If you have it made."

"Yeah. Do you want to come in?"

"Okay."

Coco followed the two of them into the kitchen, which suddenly seemed very small with Wyatt in it. He leaned up against the small butcher block island while Maggie got two cups down from the cupboard. By some kind of unspoken agreement, neither of them spoke until she had poured the coffee, added milk and two sugars to hers, milk and three sugars to his, and set it in front of him.

"Thank you," he said without looking at her. She watched him take a sip, then put the mug down.

He finally looked at her, and she tried not to breathe too noticeably. "The fire department found a piece of a device in David's bilge."

Maggie felt something that had been warm and vulnerable inside her suddenly frost over. "What kind of a device?" she asked quietly.

"Some kind of a battery, hooked up to a cell phone. I'm not really sure. ATF has it right now."

Maggie wrapped her hands around her mug to keep them from shaking. She stared at them as she took a deep breath.

"Do you know who he was working for before he quit?" Wyatt asked her.

"No," she said to her mug. "We had a...we had an understanding. I didn't ask, he didn't tell, and I didn't have to withhold."

"Who do I start asking?"

Maggie thought, then shook her head slightly. "I don't know. None of his friends were involved and he didn't hang out with people who were. He kept it...he kept it separate."

"What about his cousin?" Wyatt asked. Maggie looked up quickly. "I know about his cousin. Would he know?"

Maggie blew out a breath. "I don't know. But let me go out there and ask him."

"You can't."

"I can help, I know—"

"You can't, dammit," Wyatt snapped.

"Why not?' she snapped back.

Wyatt held up a palm. "I need you to stop thinking like a grieving widow for a moment—"

"Is that a dig?" Maggie asked, incredulous, and hurt.

"Of course not! You're in *pain*, Maggie! But I need you to think like Maggie the cop. Aside from it being a bad idea on several different levels, anything you learned would be problematic when it comes to evidence. Anything you touched or did would be tainted. Think about it. If we arrest somebody, do you want to see them walk out of court smiling when their case is dismissed?"

Maggie chewed on the corner of her lip for a moment. "No."

"Even if it was okay, I wouldn't let you anywhere near this case."

"Why not?"

"Because I'm not stupid."

Maggie looked out the kitchen window, felt her insides begin to calm, felt the adrenalin soothe her the way it energized others.

"Who's the cousin?" Wyatt asked.

"Mark Kennedy. On Avenue D." Maggie looked back at Wyatt. "Listen to me, though. Mark's not a bad person. He came back from Iraq with one less arm and proceeded to get screwed over by every agency that could help him, including and particularly the VA. He was twenty years old, with no skills other than driving."

Wyatt held up a hand and started to say something, but Maggie interrupted.

"Wyatt. He has a baby girl and a sweet wife. He grows maybe fifty pounds of pot in a year. David hasn't run it for him for at least four years."

Maggie suddenly realized, with a wave of shame and guilt, that she was defending David's cousin, but had divorced David. She knew that if she allowed herself to think about that, she'd never be able to climb back out from under it, so she pushed it away.

"All I mean is that he's not worth pursuing," she said.

"Maggie, I'm not interested in this guy," Wyatt said kindly. "But David said he got him on with some bigger guys and I need to start from there."

Maggie nodded. "Okay."

Wyatt was leaning back against the counter across from Maggie, and she wanted to go back two, three days, when she could have walked over there and leaned in and it would have felt okay. Two, three days, to when she wouldn't have needed to so badly.

"Wait," she said. "*David* told you that?"

"Yes." Wyatt sighed, suddenly looking exhausted, and looked out her kitchen window. "On our damn date," he said, so quietly she almost didn't understand it.

Maggie felt snakes slithering through her upper intestines. Small, slow-moving snakes.

"I don't understand about this battery. In the bilge?"

"Mack has a theory," Wyatt said. Mack was Mack Jennings, the captain of the Fire Department. "He thinks someone called the cell phone once the bilge was likely to have a decent amount of diesel in it. The cell sparked the battery, and…"

Maggie nodded as he trailed off. She went to the kitchen sink and dumped her coffee, just to have a reason to turn her back. She closed her eyes as she saw David smile and wave. Heard the first muffled *boom*.

Jump!

Maggie stared at the water running over her hands. "So, does that mean that whoever did this had to be at Riverfront Park?"

"Yes."

She held her hands palm down under the faucet, rinsed away emotions that did not, would not serve her now. That would not serve David or her kids. Then she turned off the water with a jerk and turned around, leaned against the sink.

"Stevenson's is picking up David's body tomorrow afternoon," she said. "His ashes will be ready for me to pick up on Saturday."

"Mike's cousin Frank didn't make it," Wyatt said, and Maggie hated herself for forgetting that anyone else had been on the boat. She put a hand up to her mouth, then coughed to hide her shame.

"What about Mike?"

"He's got a shattered leg and a lot of 2nd and 3rd degree burns," Wyatt said. "They flew him to Tallahassee. He's from Jax originally. I understand they're going to ship the cousin back there."

Maggie nodded. She and Wyatt were silent for what seemed like several minutes.

Maggie met his gaze until she grew uncomfortable. "I'm okay, Wyatt," she said.

"No, you're really not," he answered. "Your mother says you haven't slept."

"I will."

"She also says that, as far as she knows, you haven't even let yourself cry."

"You'll feel better if I fall apart?" she asked quietly.

"I'll feel better when you get some of it out, yes."

"It's not what I do."

"Why *is* that?"

"I have to take care of the kids," she said, and it was partly true.

"Then you better let somebody take care of you," he said.

Maggie needed to not think about that too much.

"The kids wanted to go to my folks'. I was going to stay here, but now...I'm going to go over there, but I want my parents to take the kids out of town. We were supposed to take David's ashes out Sunday, but it can wait. Until this is cleared up."

"That's probably not necessary, but I'm not going to say it's a bad idea, either. Do you have any thoughts?"

"No, not really. But somebody just made an example of their father."

alf an hour later, Maggie had taken a fast shower, put
on some clean jeans and a tee shirt, and shaken out
her wet hair while she packed a few items of clothing. Then she grabbed her service weapon from the
nightstand, a Glock 23, and tucked it into the holster at the
small of her back.

She carried her overnight bag down the hall, stopped
and opened the closet. It took every bit of stretch she had
to reach the Mossberg 500 on the top shelf, which is why
it was there, although she'd taught both of her kids how to
handle firearms, and not to.

She held it in the crook of her arm and reached behind
the packages of toilet paper on the second shelf, grabbed
the box of Hornady Low Recoil double-aught rounds. She
popped the action lock button, activated the safety, and
loaded two rounds. Then she locked the action again and
stuffed the Mossberg and the box of ammo into a duffel she
kept in the bottom of the closet.

She carried the two bags into the kitchen, stepped up
onto the stool by the fridge, and pulled her Grandpa's .38

revolver out of the top cupboard, grabbed a box of ammo out of a cookie tin, and dropped them both in her duffle.

She was pulling her cell phone charger out of the wall in the kitchen when she and Coco both heard a vehicle coming up the drive. Maggie zipped the duffel shut, slid it onto a low shelf in the island, and then went to look out of the window by the front door.

Bennett Boudreaux's black Mercedes sedan pulled into the gravel parking area next to Maggie's Jeep, and Boudreaux climbed out. If it had been any other time, Maggie would have appreciated the dramatic effect of the low, rumbling thunder in the distance as he shut his door.

Coco stood at attention next to her as she opened the door. They watched Boudreaux walk to the stairs, stop and look up.

"Hello, Maggie," he said.

"Hello, Mr. Boudreaux."

"I'm sorry for coming to your home uninvited and unannounced, but you didn't answer my calls."

"I haven't been answering many calls at all."

Boudreaux nodded, then looked at Coco. "Is that a Catahoula?"

"Yes. She is."

"The state dog of Louisiana, you know," he said.

"Yes." Maggie felt a light pressure on her chest. "We got her in Grand Isle seven years ago, when we were on vacation."

"Near my home," he said quietly. A brisk bit of wind came up, and ruffled his thick brown hair as he looked over at the river beyond the trees.

Maggie reached back and pulled out the back of her tee shirt, dropped it over her holster. Then she reached around and casually untucked the front. It occurred to her that she was looking at a man who might like her, but who might just as likely want to do her harm, even kill her. It then occurred to her, with some wonder, how much it would hurt her feelings if he did.

He looked up at her. "This is beautiful. This place."

"Thank you. It was my grandparents'."

He had one foot resting on the bottom step, his hands on either rail. He looked down at his foot for a moment.

Maggie bit the corner of her lip. "I'm sorry," she said.

He looked up at her and frowned. "For what?"

"For hitting you."

He regarded her with something like curiosity. "You think I'm angry because you punched me in the face?"

She shrugged one shoulder. "It's not something people do. Not to you."

"I stopped having to prove anything to anybody a long time ago," he said. "You didn't embarrass me."

"Well. I apologize," she said.

"You were in pain. Shock as well, I expect."

Maggie looked down at him as he looked around the yard. Why did she like this man? More accurately, why did she want so much for it to be okay to like him? And, after thirty-seven years of living in the same small town, passing each other on the sidewalk, or sitting on the same bay, how did he so quickly become a central character in her life? It was not her nature to be drawn to anything that might imperil her.

"Would you like to come up?" she asked anyway.

"Yes. Thank you."

She and Coco stepped out onto the front deck as Boudreaux ascended the stairs, his deck shoes only making noise when he hit the seventh step. The post beneath it had weakened or settled, and David had been planning to come replace it.

Boudreaux looked down at the tread as it wobbled. "You should get your father to fix that," he said, as he stepped onto the deck.

Coco, seeing that Maggie was okay with the stranger, wagged her back half from a seated position, and looked up at him with a semi-enthusiastic smile. Maggie could tell that Coco wanted to like him, but wasn't sure she should. Maggie understood the confusion.

She led him over to the table and chairs on the side deck. "Would you like a glass of wine?"

"If you're having one," he answered.

"I think so. It's Muscadine. Is that all right?"

"Really." He almost smiled. "That would be nice."

"Coco, stay," Maggie said, and Coco sat next to the nearest chair as Maggie walked into the house. Through the window, she saw Boudreaux sit down in the opposite chair. If her world had not turned inside out, she would have felt the oddness of his being there more keenly.

She grabbed the bottle from the counter and two glasses from the rack, and headed back out. As she did, she saw Boudreaux with his hand stretched toward Coco, and Coco with her head stretched toward his hand. They lacked four good inches to make contact.

She set the wine and glasses down on the table. "You can say hi, Coco."

Coco lifted her butt from the deck, just enough to sniff Boudreaux's hand. He smiled, scratched at the side of her head, and then Coco sat back down as Maggie sat.

Maggie poured the wine and handed Boudreaux a glass. They both took a sip. For the first time, she noticed that almost every time they had a conversation, it was accompanied by a drink. It was an anomaly for her, someone who really didn't drink that much or that often.

Boudreaux lowered his glass and cradled it in his lap, then looked beyond her somewhere. "I remember, twenty-two, twenty-three years ago, back when Craig played baseball. I loved it when his team played David's, and when they didn't, if David's team followed them or something, I would watch David's team play. He was so graceful, that kid."

Maggie took a swallow of her wine to hide a lip that threatened to tremble.

"I remember seeing you there, too," he said, and Maggie looked up at him. "Cheering him on like he was a gladiator, getting this proud little smile when he slammed one out past center field or slid into home. Getting worked up when there was a bad call."

He smiled kindly at her. "I thought it was touching."

Maggie lowered her eyes to her glass.

"I'm truly and deeply sorry, Maggie," Boudreaux said, and when she looked up, it was as though his smile had never been there. His incredible, almost impossibly blue eyes looked right through her skin and muscle and bone.

"Thank you," she almost whispered.

They stared at each other, and while it wasn't specifically uncomfortable, it was unusually intense. There were times like these, when they were alone and he looked right at her, that she was within an inch of asking him some truly honest questions. It was as though his gaze was an invitation and he would actually give her honest answers, but only if and when she asked the questions.

But there were too many, and the answers might not be what she was prepared to hear or, more accurately, act on.

"Have you been apprised of the developments regarding your ex-husband, Maggie?" he asked softly.

It took her a moment to answer. "Do you mean that David's boat was intentionally blown up?"

"Yes. I'm sorry, that is what I mean."

"How do you know that?"

He turned his glass around in his hands. "Friends."

"Law enforcement friends?"

"Some."

"Do you know who hurt David?"

"No. And you may choose to believe this or not, but I would tell you if I did."

Maggie thought that might, in fact, be true.

"But I think I know why," he added.

"Why?"

Boudreaux leaned his elbows on the table, his glass in his hands. "He paid cash for a forty thousand dollar boat."

"How do you know that?"

"He told me," Boudreaux said. "I was buying his shrimp again, just like old times."

Maggie and Wyatt had discussed that very thing, but Maggie felt the need to speak up for David. "He'd told me before that he was saving up. He also said he got a good deal from a guy in Mobile, in exchange for helping him re-build a motor."

"And he might have," Boudreaux said. "But David was a small time transporter, running moderate amounts of me-dium-grade marijuana to Gainesville, a city that pays mid-dle-of-the-pack wholesale prices."

"I thought you weren't involved in the drug business."

"I'm not. But that doesn't mean I don't do some busi-ness with people who earn some of their money that way, or know people who earn *their* money doing business with those people."

"Mr. Boudreaux," Maggie send, leaning forward. "Do you know who David was working for?"

He drummed a thumb against his glass. "It probably won't surprise you to learn that most of the middle-sized distributors of pot in Gainesville are stupid almost to the point of needing assisted living. Among the especially stupid is someone who thinks that a few thousand dollars is worth publicly blowing up the ex-husband of a cop."

Boudreaux took a drink of his wine. "I understand that, statistically, most psychotics have high IQs. However, I know of someone in Gainesville who is both psychotic and stupid. And that someone just lost a middleman."

"What kind of middleman?"

"The kind that takes delivery of product, pays the freight, then delivers the product to his boss. He, in turn, gets a nice fee for being the moron who's standing in one place at some point with both a large amount of money and a large amount of pot."

"What happened to this guy?"

"He got burned to a crisp in a 1973 Plymouth Fury." Boudreaux took another drink of his wine. "As I hear it, he had neither pot nor money with him. So, either he was killed for stealing, or he was killed so someone else could steal."

"David wouldn't kill anyone!' Maggie said.

"I wouldn't really think so. But maybe he took something. Maybe both of them did. Either way, both of them are dead."

Maggie took a deep breath and sat back in her chair. "Who is the other guy? The guy in the car?"

"His name was Myron Graham. He was killed three weeks ago."

"Do you know who he worked for?"

"Let me ask you something before I decide how to answer that question," Boudreaux said. "If I give you a name, are you going to give that information to Sheriff Hamilton or run off on your own?"

Maggie held his gaze. Maybe they would touch on some of her questions after all. "Do you think I'm the vengeful type, Mr. Boudreaux?"

"We're all the vengeful type, Maggie. And you and I have discussed the distinction between law and justice before. One isn't always more moral than the other."

Maggie thought that was pretty much another question within an answer, something Boudreaux had turned into an art.

"I have children to take care of, Mr. Boudreaux. I would hand the information over to Wyatt."

Boudreaux's eyes got a bit of a sparkle to them, for just a moment, and he leaned his chin on his hand. "Wyatt."

Maggie declined to respond to that and Boudreaux sat back. "He worked for a few people. Among them a psychotic named Rupert Fain."

Maggie stared into her wine. "I don't suppose you happened to see any of these people from Gainesville at Riverfront Park."

"No. I didn't. But I don't know that I would recognize them anyway."

Maggie looked up at him. "Why were you there? You usually don't go to 3rd of July."

"I went because Lily didn't want to go," Boudreaux said. "That's usually reason enough for me to go anywhere."

"Wyatt's wife's name was Lily."

"Yes, I know. From what I've heard, he loved her deeply, so I would say they weren't grown from the same plant."

He sat back and sighed. "Maggie, David was a good man. I liked him. I know I told you this before, that day at your son's game, but he made some bad decisions for some good reasons."

Maggie's chest hurt from how much she wanted him to take those decisions back.

He looked Maggie in the eye, and he looked almost wistful. "It's not hard to get caught up in a riptide, even if you're a strong swimmer. You just have to pay a little less attention to where you're going."

FIFTEEN

M aggie pulled onto Bluff Road, with Coco on the passenger seat and her bags in the trunk. She picked up her cell and dialed Wyatt's number.

'Hey," he answered.

"I need you to get a pen," Maggie said.

"Okay," Wyatt said after a few seconds.

"So, a few weeks ago, a guy named Myron Graham got roasted in his car in Gainesville. He worked for some psycho dealer named Rupert Fain."

"Why do you know this?"

"Just listen. So, the prevailing theory is that this guy Myron ripped Fain off, or that someone else ripped Myron off and killed him. He was the guy that David was delivering to. I think."

"Have you been talking to David's cousin? Because I'm still trying to get hold of the guy and now I'm sorta pissed, because I asked you to stay out of it."

"I did stay out of it. I haven't talked to Mark."

"So where did you get this information?"

"Someone volunteered it."

"Were you pointing anything at them?"

"Wyatt, I haven't been out of my house until this moment."

"Where are you going?"

"My parents' house. I need you to check this out, okay?"

"I am checking it out," Wyatt said. " I'm looking this guy up right—okay, so Graham, Myron, a three-time loser for possession with intent, was found melted down to laundry soap in a junk car in some warehouse district. On... the 14th."

Maggie heard Wyatt slowly tapping at his keyboard. "Does it say he worked for this guy Fain?"

"It says...known associations include Rupert Fain." Maggie heard some more tapping. "Fain, Rupert looks like a real winner. Two stretches for distribution, one for slicing up somebody's face back in 2011. Oh, and here's an interesting tidbit. Graham, Myron used to live in Eastpoint up until five years ago. In fact, he was charged with a third 'possession with' in March, 2009. Our favorite asshat, Patrick Boudreaux, was the prosecutor, but the charges were dropped due to search and seizure issues."

Maggie thought about that a minute, but there were too many things it could mean. And not mean. Patrick was the Assistant State's Attorney, and Boudreaux's older son. The other son, Craig, was a criminal defense attorney. Lots of people thought that was hilarious.

"Where'd you get it, Maggie?"

"I can't say, Wyatt. I'm sorry."

"Is it an informant?"

"Sort of."

Wyatt was quiet for a moment. Maggie honestly didn't know why she didn't want to tell him the information had come from Boudreaux.

"I really don't want this to be a problem for us," Maggie said.

"Neither do I."

"Will you let me know what you find out?"

"At this point, I'm thinking I'll let you know when it's over."

"I suppose that's fair," Maggie said, but she felt a twinge of fear that she was hurting her relationship with Wyatt before they'd had a chance to have one.

"Of course it is," he said, but not unkindly.

Maggie wasn't sure what to say to that, or what to say next at all.

"Go to your parents'," he said. "Get some damn sleep."

"They're taking the kids up to my aunt's condo in Destin. I'm just going to say goodbye."

"Maybe you should go, too."

"No. I'm coming back to work tomorrow. I'll stay out of your way, just work on Wilmette."

Wyatt was quiet so long that she was afraid he was going to force her to stay out on leave.

"Wyatt, please. With the kids gone, I'll need to stay busy until you fix this thing with David."

After a moment, Wyatt sighed. "Okay. But only if you get some sleep first. You're in no shape to be working a case."

"I will."

"You can call me if you need to," he said quietly.

"I'll do that, too," she said.

She disconnected the call, and took a big swallow of the coffee she'd brought with her.

It had been almost three days since she'd slept, and she could feel her reasoning and her focus slipping. Wyatt was right. She was in no shape for anything. She just didn't know how to stop.

⚓ ⚓ ⚓

When Maggie got to her parents' home, she spent several minutes holding and talking to her kids. Then they all sat down at the kitchen table, and Maggie explained what she knew about what had happened to David. She had thought telling her children she'd asked their Dad to leave was the hardest thing she'd ever done. But telling them that he'd been stolen from them was immeasurably harder.

Georgia was the first one to speak when Maggie finished.

"I'm going to say one thing," she said. "I don't believe David hurt anybody."

"I don't either, Mom."

"I don't think he stole anything, either," Georgia said.

"Well, I bet you never thought he'd start running drugs for people, either," Sky said quietly.

Maggie frowned as Georgia's eyes teared. "Sky!"

Sky looked apologetically at her grandmother. "I'm sorry, Grandma. I didn't mean it like that," she said. "It's just all so freaking crazy."

She looked down at her oddly silent phone on the table, and Maggie saw her blinking away tears. "I remember when my dad was just a normal guy. He went to work every night and he came back every morning. He was a shrimper."

"He was a shrimper when he died, too, baby, and don't you forget it," Georgia said, placing a hand on Sky's. "He was a shrimper."

Gray cleared his throat. "We should get on the road. We'll take your mother's car. Sky, Kyle, why don't you take your bags out to the garage, huh? Then we'll say our good-byes."

After the kids had gone down the hall to the bedrooms, Gray looked at Maggie.

"I understand why you're not coming, Maggie, but I don't like it."

"Do you think the kids understand?"

They do," Georgia said. "Sky does."

Maggie felt the weight of guilt press on her as she thought of her little boy, mourning one parent while the other sent him away.

Gray laid a hand on top of his daughter's. "You take care of this business, and we'll take care of them. Then we'll be home."

A few minutes later, Maggie pressed each child to her in turn, then made them get in the car before she could decide it was okay for them to stay.

Once she couldn't see the car anymore, or her children's heads in the back of it, Maggie smacked the button for the garage door, and she and Coco watched it go down. The house was painfully empty when Maggie went back inside. She hadn't been alone there since she was a teenager. Everyone she loved had been there just a moment ago, and the silence they'd left her in was deafening.

She made sure that her dad had locked all the windows and the door out to the deck, then Coco followed her down the hall to the bedrooms. Maggie couldn't help but slow down along the way.

One entire wall of the hallway was covered with family photos. Maggie in first grade, one front tooth missing. Sky in first grade right next to it, missing both front teeth. Maggie and David at eleven, standing in the back of Daddy's oyster skiff with their arms around each other's shoulders. Prom night, David in the gray tux that he'd slowly disassembled throughout the evening. Maggie and David holding newborn Skylar Nicole. Maggie, David and little Sky with newborn Kyle Gray.

Maggie stopped in front of a picture that had always been her favorite, but that she had learned not to see in recent years. David and Daddy sitting on the dock out back, David playing his guitar, and Gray smiling behind his harmonica.

Maggie breathed in through her nose, and slowly out her mouth, then walked into her old bedroom, now the room where the Kyle stayed when the kids slept over. She took her service weapon out of the holster on her back, set it on the nightstand, and then sat down on the edge of the bed. Coco whined, and Maggie patted the bed. Coco jumped up and sat next to her.

The house was completely silent, except for the ticking of the AC as it shut down. But the photos out in the hallway suddenly had their own brand of loudness. If Coco hadn't been there, Maggie would have sworn she was completely alone in the world.

She picked her weapon up again and walked out of the room.

⚓   ⚓   ⚓

Maggie sat in the car, her head back on the headrest, eyes closed. Coco sat in the passenger seat, her nose pointed at the small gap in her window, sniffing at the unfamiliar surroundings and the metallic scent of forthcoming rain. Gentle thunder rumbled in the distance, and Maggie could hear the dry rustle of palm fronds along the driveway.

She heard Coco whine just a little, and Maggie reached over and put a hand on one of her paws. Then a gentle tap on her window made her jump.

Wyatt was standing at her door. She pressed the button to roll her window all the way down and looked at him, her eyes hollow and circled with shadows. Wyatt reached in and opened her door, held out his hand. She took it and let him pull her out of the Jeep, and Coco jumped out behind her.

Wyatt led them to the open front door as the first few fat drops of rain hit the walkway, giving off the telltale, uniquely Floridian scent of newly dampened hot concrete. Maggie walked inside, but Coco half sat on the doormat, her butt inches from the floor, her nose inches from the threshold. Wyatt patted his thigh and she trotted in.

Maggie was sitting on the rattan couch with the blue striped cushions, and Coco went and sat next to the coffee table. Wyatt walked over and sat down beside Maggie and, when she looked at him, her eyes were full of defeat. He lifted an arm and she leaned in, put her head on his shoulder.

They sat there for a moment, and then the tears began to fall. As soon as she felt them on her face, Maggie lost her grip on the reins holding her grief. Sounds came up from her gut that were not unlike the sounds she'd made giving birth to her children, and it frightened and embarrassed her. Coco laid her face on Maggie's knee and cried quietly with her.

Maggie put her hands over her face, but Wyatt gently reached up and took her hands away, then pulled her to his chest. She buried her face there and felt twenty-two years of careful control come up out of her soul.

$$ \updownarrow \quad \updownarrow \quad \updownarrow $$

A few hours later, Maggie was sound asleep. Wyatt was stretched out on the couch, Maggie still cradled on his chest. Coco slept on top of Wyatt's feet, her head on Maggie's hip.

The rain had stayed for the night, and drummed on the roof, almost drowning out the gentle chime on Maggie's phone, where it rested on the coffee table next to her .45. Wyatt reached over and flipped it open, saw that the text was from Sky.

We're here. Are you okay?

Wyatt balanced the phone behind Maggie's back and carefully thumbed a reply. *It's Wyatt. Your Mom's asleep on my couch.*

After a moment, he thought maybe she wouldn't answer. But then the phone chimed again.

Good.

CHAPTER
SIXTEEN

A melia opened the front door to find Patrick Boudreaux on the steps.

Patrick was in his early forties, and good looking in a way that men trying very hard can be. His suits were custom tailored, his dark hair perfectly barbered and shiny with gel, and he got weekly manicures from the Vietnamese ladies at a shop in Panama City. He was the type of man who is impressive to those who are easily impressed.

"Yes?"" Amelia asked, obviously not among the easily impressed.

"He asked to see me," Patrick said, looking irritated.

Amelia opened the door wider and Patrick stepped in. "He's havin' his coffee out back," she said, and closed the door behind him.

Patrick headed through the living room off of the front hall. "Would you bring me some coffee, please?" he asked over his shoulder.

Amelia was already headed back to the kitchen. "Naw, she said. "Don't work for no *couillion.*"

Boudreaux was sitting at the white wrought iron table on the back porch, looking crisp and fresh, despite the already searing sun, and the thick, damp air. He was on his third cup of chicory coffee when Patrick stepped out through the French doors from the living room.

He sat down at the table across from Boudreaux, jerking his arms to straighten his sleeves.

"You summoned?" Patrick asked as though he were only half-interested in an answer.

Boudreaux blinked slowly as he stared at Patrick, and Patrick finally broke his gaze by looking down at his hand. "You would do well to distance yourself from Rupert Fain," Boudreaux said.

Patrick looked back up at him, spread his hands. "What's this about?"

"You told me, with Myron gone to his great reward, that you were going to start dealing with Fain directly. I suggest that you don't."

Patrick swallowed, and a hard look came into his eyes. "What's going on?"

"The police are looking at him."

"The police are always looking at him."

"They're looking at him for David Seward's murder."

Patrick looked at Boudreaux for a long moment, his eyes flat, as Boudreaux took a sip of his coffee. "Why would they be doing that?" he asked, his voice cold and hard.

"Because Myron Graham got turned into a pile of S'mores in his car."

"Why would they even connect the two? How do they—Seward told his little wife about Myron."

"No, I did."

Patrick stared at him, his eyes wide. Boudreaux seemed unconcerned, took another drink of his coffee.

"What the hell possessed you to do that?"

"Watch your tone, Patrick," he said calmly.

"What is this *thing* with you and that woman?"

"I'm working on something."

Patrick started to sputter, then just grinned. "Working on what? Having another friend in the SO? Because you've got the wrong cop for that, old man."

"If it was any of your business, I would have already told you."

"It is my business. What is it with her?" he asked, his voice rising. Boudreaux just stared at him. "Are you—do you have the *hots* for Maggie Redmond?"

"I'll ignore that question," Boudreaux answered.

"Look what the hell you're doing! Look at what you've done!" Patrick pinched at the bridge of his nose. "You're going to ruin this family!"

Boudreaux leaned forward, and Patrick instinctively sat back.

"Killing David Seward was wrong," Boudreaux said evenly. "I don't think he stole anything. He was too damn proud of having saved up for that boat. Myron Graham made his bed and he burned up in it, but I don't think Seward helped him steal Fain's product."

"No, he didn't, Pop." Patrick was laughing softly, but without humor. "I did."

Boudreaux stared at Patrick for a long moment. "What the hell did you do?" he asked quietly.

"Myron's been whining about not paying me my stipend anymore, the other guys have dropped off in volume, and I'm going damn broke," Patrick snapped.

"*What* did you do?"

"I took the damn pot, what do you think I did?" Patrick jerked upright and leaned over the table. "He'd told me he was taking a delivery that Saturday, and that I could come get my last cut. He said he wasn't worried about some pissant little drug charge anymore, because I had more to lose."

Boudreaux took a long slow breath and let it out. "So you let Seward and this guy Myron take the fall for it."

"No, I let Seward take the fall for all of it, including Myron."

Boudreaux telegraphed nothing. One moment he was sitting calmly with his hand on his coffee, and the next moment the reddening imprint of his palm was on Patrick's meticulously shaven cheek.

"You are a raging imbecile," Boudreaux said quietly. "If you were my flesh and blood, I'd be ashamed."

"Why? Because you've never killed anyone, Pop? I learned at your feet! And it really wasn't that hard."

Boudreaux's blue eyes were cold and hard. "I don't destroy families for money."

"You're gonna destroy this one for a roll in the hay, though, right?"

Boudreaux stood up slowly. Patrick was quicker about it.

"You made a bad decision, Patrick," Boudreaux said quietly. "Live with the consequences. Or don't."

"What's that supposed to mean? I promise you, if they nail Fain and he talks about me, I'm talking about you."

"Understand this more clearly than you have ever understood anything. You wouldn't live long enough to keep that promise."

Boudreaux walked away from the table, opened the door to the kitchen, and shut it quietly behind him.

Patrick turned around to leave and stopped short when he saw his mother standing at the French door to the living room. He grabbed his sunglasses from the table and went inside.

"What's going on, Patrick?" Lily Boudreaux asked. Her artificially arched brows were at attention.

"Nothing."

"Who is this person that might say things about you?"

"Nobody, Mother. Stay out of it, please."

"Why is he so angry?"

"Look, why don't you ask him? While you're at it, why don't you ask him about Maggie Redmond?"

"What about her?"

"I think the old man's actually in love with her."

Lily let out a sharp laugh. "Patrick. He's in love with no one. If he's interested in that trawler trash, it's either entirely sexual or he wants something more valuable from her. Let him have her."

"She's trouble."

"Everybody's trouble, son."

SEVENTEEN

Maggie woke up to Coco licking and nuzzling her hand. It took her a minute to realize she wasn't at home, and when she opened her eyes, she found she was still on Wyatt's couch.

She slowly sat up, feeling achy, abused, and hung over. Wyatt was nowhere in sight, and the house was quiet. But Maggie smelled coffee. She got up and walked barefooted to the breakfast bar in the kitchen, where a full pot of coffee sat, a mug and spoon beside it. Under the mug was a note. Wyatt had gone to Gainesville. Coco had peed and eaten leftover stew. The security code was 4098.

Maggie poured the coffee and opened the fridge to get some milk. A Tetris game of take-out containers filled most of the fridge. Beer, wine, Mountain Dew and steak filled out the remainder of Wyatt's food supply. Maggie made a mental note to feed him.

She drank her coffee as she walked around the house, Coco trailing behind her, soundless on the cream-colored carpet. Down the hall from the living room was a small bedroom that Wyatt apparently used as an office. There was a computer on a small desk, and one wall was covered in bookshelves. Maggie took a brief look at the books. Some Hemingway, some John Sandford. What looked like every single James Lee Burke. At the end of one shelf was a picture of a quietly pretty blond woman, smiling into the sun. Lily Hamilton. The sight of her made Maggie feel guilty for being there, and she turned to go.

When she did, she saw another framed photo on a side table. Wyatt, Dwight, James from Narcotics, and Dwight's brother Rob, the day two years prior, when a bunch of them went out to lunch to celebrate Wyatt's forty-sixth birthday. Maggie was saying something to Wyatt, and Wyatt was leaning in and laughing. She wondered what it was she had said.

Maggie wandered back out to the hallway, found and used the masculine but clean bathroom, poked her head into a guest room, then stood in Wyatt's bedroom doorway. Two of the pillows were missing from one side of the made bed. Maggie assumed they were the ones she'd woken up on. The room reminded her of a vacation rental, only less impersonal. A framed vintage poster for the Cocoa Beach Pier hung above the bed, and a rattan lounge sat under one window, a paperback book open and upside down on the small table beside it.

Maggie suddenly felt invasive and improper, and she and Coco walked back to the kitchen to get one more cup of coffee for the road.

⚓ ⚓ ⚓

Rather than drive all the way back out to her house, Maggie showered and changed at her parents' home, and put Coco in the fenced back yard with some food and water.

She was about to head to her car when her cell phone rang. It was the office.

"Hello?"

"Hey, uh, Maggie, it's Dwight."

"Hey, Dwight."

"Hey. I'm real sorry about David. Real sorry," he said.

"Thank you. What's up, Dwight?"

"Well, we got a call few minutes ago, guy named Mitch Fallon, moved here a couple years ago from Alabama?"

"I don't think I know him."

"Well, anyway, he saw the foot guy's picture on the TV, you know when Channel 10 came down to talk to Wyatt?"

"I didn't know Wyatt talked to the news about it."

"Yeah. Well, uh...it was the 4th of July."

"Okay."

"Anyway, Fallon says he saw the foot guy down by the docks when he was heading out that Tuesday night. He's a shrimper, too."

"Really." Maggie turned around in a circle, looking for her keys, before she realized that she'd left them in her car. "How do I get in touch with him?"

"He's down there now. Replacing one of the catheads on his boat."

"Okay, where?"

"Number 14, over at Boudreaux's."

"Huh. Okay, thanks, Dwight."

Maggie had almost headed for Café con Leche to pick up a double, but it was practically across the street from Riverfront Park and she just couldn't do it. She ended up going the long way around to get to the marina, then sat in the sweltering car for a full five minutes before she could get out.

She made a point of not looking in the direction of the dock where she had gone out in search of David, the dock she'd returned to after she'd found him. Instead, she focused on the keys in her hand as she headed right toward slip #14.

Mitch Fallon was a short, stocky man of about fifty, with a Crimson Tide cap covering an almost bald head. When Maggie stopped at the slip, Mitch was squatting next to an open toolbox, wiping down a long wrench with a blue shop towel.

"Mr. Fallon?" Maggie asked.

He looked up, then stood. "Yes, ma'am," he answered, in a distinctively coastal Alabama accent.

"I'm Lt. Redmond from the Sheriff's Office."

"Yes, ma'am," he said again.

"I understand you think you saw Brandon Wilmette Tuesday the 24th?"

"Yeah."

"You recognized him from a picture on TV?"

"Yeah. I was going to call right away, but I...uh...I was a little nervous about it."

"Why's that?"

Fallon glanced over his shoulder toward the Sea-Fair building. "Well, I mean, I sell shrimp over there, you know what I mean?"

Maggie nodded. "Yeah, I understand. What time did you see him?"

"I'm not real sure what time it was. It was close on to dusk, though. I was underway by ten. I got out late. Had some trouble with my winch."

"Okay. Where did you see him, exactly?"

"He was going in around back, to Sea-Fair. Knocked on the back door."

"Did someone open it?"

"Yes, ma'am, but I couldn't tell who, from this angle. But a little while later, Mr. Boudreaux came out the back."

"How much later?"

"I'm not sure. Sorry. But it couldn't have been more than a half hour before I shoved off."

"You didn't see the other man come out?"

"No, I didn't. I'm not saying he didn't, but I didn't see it. Course, I was working on the winch."

Maggie looked over toward the Sea-Fair offices. Only a small slice of the front parking lot was visible from where she stood. "Did you happen to see Wilmette drive up?"

"Naw, sorry. I only turned around 'cause I heard him knocking on the door."

"Okay." Maggie bit the corner of her lip. "How did Mr. Boudreaux look when he came out?"

"How do you mean?"

"Well, was he rushing, did he look upset or anything?"

Fallon looked uncomfortable for a moment. "No, not really. He just walked out to the front parking lot there."

"Did you hear a car?"

"No, but there was a bunch of noise from over at Up the Creek. I think they had a game on."

"Okay." Maggie nodded. "Anything else you can think of?"

"Not really, ma'am. That's pretty much it. I really only remembered it 'cause I didn't have no crew that night. I remember seeing the guy and thinking I'd even take him, just to have another body. Well, you know what I mean."

"Why *even* him?"

Fallon shrugged a shoulder. "Well, I mean he looked like a city boy. I doubt he had a callous anywhere on him."

Maggie nodded again, thanked the man, and headed back to her car. On her way there, she saw Boudreaux's black Mercedes parked in front of the Sea-Fair office, and she veered that way and walked through the glass front door.

The office area was nothing fancy, though it was respectable. An attractive, dishwater-blond woman who looked like the perfect soccer Mom sat behind an equally dishwater-blond reception desk.

She smiled up at Maggie as she walked in. "Good morning. May I help you?" She seemed to recognize or read the SO logo on Maggie's polo shirt after the fact, and her smile faltered just a bit, not from fear, just from surprise.

"Yes, please," Maggie answered with a polite smile she was surprised to manage. "I need to speak with Mr. Boudreaux for a minute."

"Oh. Certainly," the blond said. "He's over in the new processing plant. If you'll have a seat, I'll call him."

"Actually, could you just take me to him?"

The woman's smile flickered, as she thought about whether it was okay. "Well, I...he usually talks to people in his office."

"It's okay," Maggie said. "We're pals."

The woman looked back at her for a moment, then seemed to decide that this matter wasn't going to benefit her from either direction, and was best gotten off her hands. She stood up and straightened her beige khaki skirt. "If you'll come with me."

Maggie followed the woman down a tiled hallway and through three turns before the hallway turned to concrete and they came to a brand-new looking steel door. The woman looked over her shoulder at Maggie, then depressed the bar to open the door.

Looking over the woman's shoulder, Maggie saw a cavernous room, and industrial-looking spray hoses hanging from the ceiling in evenly spaced rows. The woman set one tan pump inside the room and bent to insert her torso.

After a moment, she raised a hand, and a moment later, Boudreaux appeared in the door way. "Yes, Patty?"

"Sir, this officer is here to see you," Patty said hesitantly.

Maggie stepped to the side just a bit and Boudreaux raised his chin at her.

"Hello, Maggie."

"Good morning, Mr. Boudreaux."

Patty looked from one to the other of them, and Boudreaux seemed to wait for some explanation for Maggie's presence. Patty seemed to hope she'd give one, too.

"I just stopped by to talk to you for a minute, if that's okay," Maggie said. "I'm sorry to bother you at work."

Boudreaux nodded. "Yes, that's fine. It's good to see you.' He looked at Patty, who scurried back the way they'd come, and Boudreaux held the door open wider. "Would you like to see the new addition to the company?"

"Sure," she answered, and stepped inside.

Several people, men and women, stood at two rows of stainless steel tables, scaling and fileting fish. Maggie could see clear plastic bins of redfish, sea trout, and snapper.

"We've expanded to include fish, as you can see," Boudreaux said. "It's good for business, of course, with the oyster and shrimp yields down, but it's a handful of new jobs, as well. We're selling fresh and frozen, to the supermarkets, to restaurants."

Maggie looked at the far end of the room, where a tall, thin man at one of the tables was hosing down his station. The pinkish water slid across the floor, and swirled around and down one of several floor drains.

"Let's head up there to the office," Boudreaux said, pointing to a set of metal stairs that led to an office with a wall of windows.

"Okay," Maggie said, and looked around as she followed Boudreaux across the room and up the stairs. The faint smell of some expensive cologne she didn't recognize wafted down to her as she climbed the steps behind Boudreaux, and she thought, not for the first time, what an odd mix of blue collar and effortless class he was.

As she understood it, he'd worked on his father's shrimp boats and oyster skiffs back in Louisiana, and here as well, when his father expanded to Apalach. Then he'd gone on to get a finance degree at Ole Miss, built his own businesses in Louisiana, and come here when his father had died. He'd taken the wholesale business and shrimp fleets his father had left and built a multi-million dollar business that included seafood processing, vacation rentals, vessel leasing and who knew what else.

If nothing else, she admired his work ethic and business sense. But there was something else she liked, as well, something she didn't yet want to define very specifically.

Boudreaux opened the office door, and held a hand out to indicate she should sit in one of the vinyl armchairs. "Have a seat. Please."

He closed the door as she sat down, then he took a seat behind the inexpensive oak desk that afforded a view of almost the entire room downstairs.

The office was spare and looked unlived in. There was a computer on the ell of the desk, a table with a potted plant, a brand new phone. No artwork, no rugs, no stacks of files or half-full coffee mugs.

Boudreaux watched her looking around as he leaned back in the brown leather desk chair. "This was supposed to be Gregory's office," he said.

Maggie glanced at him, then swallowed a tinge of nausea and occupied her eyes elsewhere for a moment. "Brandon Wilmette's as well?"

"It would have been, yes." He gently rubbed at one eyebrow with a slender finger. "Has our discussion yesterday been helpful?"

"I passed the information on to Wyatt. Thank you." She looked at him. "For obvious reasons, I can't actually have anything to do with the case."

Boudreaux nodded. Then he waited for her to speak.

"We got a call from someone who saw Brandon Wilmette here the evening of Tuesday the 24th. The day before he disappeared."

"Yes. As I told you, he came by here that evening."

"Do you remember what time?"

"I told him to come any time after seven, but no, I don't remember when he arrived."

Maggie nodded. "Do you remember what time he left?"

Boudreaux rubbed his eyebrow again. It was a habit that Maggie had noted lately. He seemed to do it when he was thinking. "Not really, no. He left before I did. I had some paperwork to finish up. But I left around ten, I think."

"You don't have any idea how long you'd been here after he left?"

Boudreaux put his elbows on the desk and folded his hands. "An hour perhaps? Maybe a little bit longer."

"So, kind of a long conversation, then."

"With Sport, every conversation was a long one, no matter how brief it was." He rested his chin on his hands. "First we talked about Gregory, or I listened to him talk about Gregory. Then he went into a long, but unconvincing pitch for some pop-up gourmet business back in Atlanta. I declined to invest."

"And then you offered him a job?"

"Gregory's job," Boudreaux said, and she wondered if he mentioned Gregory's name so frequently in order to get a reaction from her.

"Why?"

"He was a dumbass, please excuse the language, but he'd been a friend of the family for a long time. I also didn't have anyone to fill the position right away. I still didn't, up until last week. One of the shrimpers' wives used to work for the Publix seafood department. She'll be taking over for me Monday."

"Did you and Wilmette discuss your nephew's suicide? Did he have any thoughts as to why he might kill himself?"

"Not really, no. Sport didn't get distracted much by other people's feelings or mental states." His eyes had taken on that speculative look he sometimes got, and she worked at not looking away. "You never met him, never saw him around town with Gregory?"

Maggie swallowed, tried to make it unnoticeable, but she saw that he noticed. "Your nephew wasn't around much in recent years."

"No, but when he was here, Sport joined him fairly often." He was still staring, though not in a way meant to intimidate. It did, nonetheless.

Maggie pushed past it and decided to get a few things out in the open.

"How long had he been coming here?" She wanted an answer, but almost hoped he'd decline to give one.

"The first time he came down was when he and Gregory were freshman at Tulane. I think it was fall break." He was still watching her.

"That would have been...?"

"Twenty-two years ago," he said, like it had always been on the tip of his tongue.

Maggie looked down at the car keys in her hand for a second, just to break that gaze for a moment. Then she faced him again. She was trying to think of what to say next when he spoke.

"I suppose you would have been too young to have known them, really," he said quietly.

"I was fifteen," she said. "But I knew who your nephew was."

"But you don't recall meeting Sport?"

Hey, you want some?

"I don't remember ever seeing him, no," she answered, and she knew that they both knew they were now having a completely different conversation. She knew he was confirming for her, more directly this time, that Brandon Wilmette had been the other person in the woods that day. What she didn't know was why he would do that. Why, after twenty-two years, would he care to impart that information?

She stood up, and he stood with her, looking a little surprised that she'd decided to leave. "Thank you. Mr. Boudreaux. I'll let you get back to work."

"Maggie?" She stopped and turned, one hand on the door knob. "I'm terribly sorry," he said.

Maggie looked at hm a moment. "For what?"

"Everything," he said.

Maggie nodded and went out the door.

As she went back down the stairs to the processing room, she looked around at the stainless steel and the hoses and the drains. It was a place built specifically for messy work. A perfect place to chop up a body. As she came off the bottom step, she realized that she really didn't want it to be.

CHAPTER
EIGHTEEN

Maggie spent the next few hours talking on the phone to people in Atlanta, trying to find some kind of motive, any kind of motive, for the murder of Brandon Wilmette. Anything that did not involve Bennett Boudreaux. She came up empty. Wilmette was not liked by many, and he was even despised by a few, but there was nothing in his life that pointed to a motive for someone to follow him all the way to Apalach to kill him.

What she was left with was the same thing she'd had when she'd started, a near certainty in her gut that Wilmette had tried to blackmail Boudreaux with the fact that his nephew had once raped hometown girl and decorated Sheriff's Lieutenant Maggie Redmond. How Wilmette planned to handle having his bluff called, when he would be at minimum an accessory, was beyond Maggie's understanding, but she figured his bluff *had* been called, just in an unexpected way.

When the phone calls had been exhausted, Maggie drove around the marinas, walked downtown, visited Caroline's and went back to the Bayview, hoping to find someone who had seen Wilmette after 10 p.m. on Tuesday the 24th. Again, she came up empty. A few people remembered seeing him beforehand, no one remembered seeing him after.

At close to six, she decided to call it a day, pick up Coco, and head home. She pulled into the gas station first, pulled up to one of the pumps, and set the pump to fill the tank while she went inside to grab a cold drink. She automatically reached for the RC, but stopped short, then grabbed a can of Dr. Pepper instead.

As she walked out of the station, she saw Patrick Boudreaux getting gas on the other side of her pump. He was leaning up against the side of his blue Audi, texting on his phone. He looked up as she approached, and seemed taken aback for just a split second, before he managed to locate his usual arrogant expression.

"Hello, Maggie."

Maggie continued past him to her side of the pump. "Hello, Patrick."

She popped her Dr. Pepper and waited for the last few gallons of gas to pump.

"I was sorry to hear about your ex-husband. Terrible thing."

His statement carried so little sincerity that Maggie didn't feel obligated to thank him. Normally, she tried to have a civil relationship with Patrick, since she depended on him to prosecute most of her cases. She did this despite the fact that she was sure his inconsistent results were due to inconsistencies in his ethics. For his part, Patrick had never treated her with anything other than polite, smirking disdain. Patrick didn't seem to care for women in law enforcement.

Maggie looked back over at Patrick, who had returned to his texting. "Patrick, do you remember Myron Graham?"

For a moment, she'd thought he hadn't heard her. But his thumbs had stopped moving. Finally, he looked up, his eyebrows clenched together in thought.

"Doesn't ring a bell, I'm afraid," he said. "Who is he?"

"A drug dealer. Pot. PD arrested him in 2009 for possession with intent. It was assigned to you."

"I can't say I recall. What about it?"

"He's dead."

Patrick looked back down at his phone. Maggie's pump had stopped. So had Patrick's.

"Well, I guess that's one less dealer we need to worry about," Patrick said to his phone.

"Well, he's one less problem for somebody." Maggie replaced the pump in its holder and grabbed her receipt. "They found him burned to a crisp in Gainesville."

Patrick glanced up as though he'd just heard his pump stop. "No. I don't care about Alachua County."

He stuck his phone in his back pocket and pulled the pump from his tank.

"You don't care much about Franklin County, either," she said.

He turned around, jammed the pump into place. "What the hell is that supposed to mean?"

"It's not self-explanatory?"

"Maybe you could explain it to my father," he said, and tried for a snide smile.

"I don't usually have to explain things to your father," she said, and was more successful with her smile than he had been with his.

He put an elbow on top of the pump, and leaned over her. "Listen, I don't care what kind of crap you're playing with the old man. Maybe you think you have a real romance going or maybe you're just pulling his chain. Maybe he's pulling yours."

"You think I'm sleeping with your father?" Maggie asked, incredulous. She couldn't help but laugh just a little.

"I don't know and I don't care," Patrick said. "But don't come at me with your sanctimonious BS, because I don't buy it."

"I'm not in a relationship with your father," she said evenly. "But I'll tell you what, he's twice the man you are on his worst day."

Patrick leaned in again. "You keep thinking that. But *I'll* tell *you* this. Bennett Boudreaux never met anyone he didn't think was disposable."

⚓   ⚓   ⚓

Maggie picked up Coco and her things and went on home. She returned her guns to their normal locations, fed the chickens, fed Coco, and took a hot shower, then went out onto the deck with Coco and a glass of wine.

Dark clouds crept by, low to the ground, but it looked to Maggie like they were going to head out to sea before they finally broke. However, the attending light breeze was welcome.

Maggie's cell rang, and she saw that it was Wyatt.

"Hey," she said.

"Hey. How are you?"

"I'm doing okay. Better," she said. "Are you back?"

"No, I was calling to let you know that I'm still in Gainesville. Alachua County's trying to help us track down Fain, but it's like he's vaporized."

"Have you learned anything new?"

"Only that Myron Graham was stabbed to death prior to being roasted, and that Fain is suspected in another murder from a couple of years ago, some girl who used to deal for him." Wyatt sighed. He sounded exhausted. "Dwight said you were in the office today."

"Yeah. I made some calls to Atlanta, but nobody had anything to say that would point to a motive for murder. I also canvassed the marina and downtown, but no one remembers seeing Wilmette after Tuesday evening."

"So nothing new on the foot."

"Well, I talked to a shrimper who saw Wilmette go into Sea-Fair Tuesday night, but we already knew he'd been there."

Maggie felt a pang of guilt at neglecting to mention her conversation with Boudreaux, but going too much into Boudreaux meant going into Gregory as well, and she didn't know how to do that. A small voice in her head mentioned that her reasons for staying silent were selfish and unethical, but she shut it out.

Just then, Stoopid, so known mainly due to his lack of ability to tell time, let out one of his odd half-crows from under the deck.

"Is that Stoopid?" Wyatt asked.

"Yeah."

"Are all of your chickens in my yard?"

"No, I'm at home."

"Why? Why the hell do you think I gave you the code to my security system?"

"So I could lock up."

"And so you could come back," he snapped. "Even if I'm not home yet, my house is a better place for you at the moment than yours."

"I had to feed my chickens, anyway, Wyatt," Maggie said. "Besides, the threat might be serious enough to get my kids out of town, but it's not enough to warrant any real worry for me."

"I don't know that I agree or disagree, but it's still not a good idea for you to be out in the middle of nowhere by yourself."

"I'm usually out in the middle of nowhere by myself."

"This isn't usually," Wyatt said quietly. "You need to take precautions, and by taking precautions I mean not be an idiot."

Maggie sighed. "I'm fine, Wyatt. Are you coming back tonight?"

"At some point. We'll probably leave it to Alachua in a couple hours, if none of these leads on Fain's whereabouts pan out. Do you want me to come by?"

"No, I'll probably be asleep."

"Then I'll call."

Maggie couldn't help smiling. "All right," she said.

"If you need me, call."

"I will," Maggie said.

"I almost believe you," Wyatt said.

⚓ ⚓ ⚓

Maggie's face was pressed hard into the dirt and three inches of musty autumn leaves. Sticks and at least one rock cut into her left cheek.

The ground, and the weight on her back, made it hard for her to breathe. She was sure that her heart was pounding too hard to let her live, and her chest was on fire. Everything was on fire and yet she was so cold.

"Tell me you love me!" he said, his hot breath blowing like a dragon's on her right ear.

She kept her lips tightly shut, her nostrils flaring as she tried to get enough air without opening her mouth. She could see her fishing rod a few feet away where she'd dropped it, the one Daddy had given her for getting straight A's last semester. He didn't know where she was, didn't know she needed him, and she closed her eyes as hot tears flooded them again.

"Tell me you love me!" he insisted again. She felt another sharp pain and her mouth flew open. She intended to tell him what he wanted to hear, but suddenly her throat felt like someone had scraped it with a nail file. She didn't hear, didn't even realize she was screaming, until the weight came off of her and she heard him yell "Shut up!"

He flipped her over roughly and she felt herself getting ready to scream again, against her own will. The sight of him stopped her. His shirt was hanging open, his pants around his thighs, and he was holding a rock the size of a basketball over his head.

She was fifteen and nobody knew she was way back in the woods. She was going to die in the dirt and the moldy leaves, and Daddy's heart was going to break.

She clamped a hand over her own mouth and willed herself not to scream anymore.

Gregory Boudreaux slammed the rock down right next to her head and laughed. Then he leaned down to kiss her neck.

She clamped her hand so tightly over her mouth that she could feel the outline of every one of her upper teeth on her lip. In her left hand, she squeezed a clump of rocks and twigs.

She couldn't seem to breathe fast or deeply enough and the air whistled out of her nostrils with every exhale.

He was kissing her neck sloppily as he crushed her spine into the dirt and rocks, and she kept herself from retching by staring up at the treetops. It was dark down there on the ground, but the late afternoon autumn sky was brilliant blue and cloudless, as though everything was alright everywhere else.

Gregory raised up onto his knees and blocked her view of the real world. He looked off to the left and smiled.

"You want some?" he asked.

*Maggie turned her head to the right, and there, standing be-
neath the trees, was Brandon Wilmette, holding his own de-
cayed and swollen foot.*

Maggie bolted upright in bed, her chest heaving, her
tank top covered in sweat. Coco jumped down as Maggie
threw off the covers and put her feet on the floor. She took
a few deep breaths, then grabbed her cell phone and her
service weapon from the nightstand, and walked out into
the living room. Coco's tags jingled as she followed.

Maggie took a quick look around the living room,
checked the locks on the windows and made sure the dead-
bolt was locked. She did these things, even though she'd
done them before she'd gone to bed, because that was what
she did when she had the nightmares. Fear didn't require
things to make sense.

She walked into the kitchen, got a glass of water from
the tap, and drank it down. Then she got another. She
made a point of not catching her reflection in the window
over the sink. Then she rinsed out the glass, walked back to
the main room, and sat down at the cypress table.

Before the day Gregory Boudreaux's body had been
found on the beach, she hadn't had a nightmare in two
years. She'd never had one in which she saw Brandon Wilmette, and she knew that it was dream, not memory. She
had never looked into the trees. In fact, until two weeks
ago, she'd never even remembered that Gregory had spoken to someone else that day.

Maggie absently stroked Coco's neck and looked at her
cell phone. Wyatt had called just before she'd gone to bed,
and she was tempted to call him back, tempted to tell him
she was on her way. She just couldn't.

She would have no problem going to Wyatt's or her parents if she'd been worried about Fain or whoever it was

that had hurt David. But she would not run one inch for Gregory Boudreaux.

Maggie woke late for her. It was her day off, according to the monthly schedule, though she was still technically on bereavement leave.

She had her first cup of coffee in the shower, willing the steaming water to ease her muscles, cramped from stress and lack of sleep, while the caffeine cleared the dust from her neurons.

After she got dressed, she fed the chickens and let Coco run around to do her business, then she filled Coco's bowls on the front deck, leaned on the railing, and stared at David's truck as she drank her second cup of coffee.

She found several things to do instead of the things that she knew needed to be done. She cleaned the chicken coop. She picked cucumbers, beans, and overgrown zucchinis from her raised beds, throwing much of the produce into the chicken yard because it was past its prime. She mopped her floors and did some laundry.

In between all of these chores, she stood at the deck rail, drinking more coffee or a glass of tea, and stared at David's truck while Coco sat beside her.

Finally, late in the afternoon, she grabbed David's keys from a hook by the door, left Coco on the deck with an apology, and climbed into David's truck.

There was still a trace of Jovan Musk in the cab, and the indentation in the worn driver's seat made Maggie unbearably sad. She shifted herself into it, settled her backside into the dip that David had created over the years, moved her right leg so that her legs fit inside the two slight grooves. Then she took a deep breath and let it go ahead and tear at her. She gave the pain a few moments to roam freely, then adjusted the seat forward with a jerk, started the truck, adjusted the mirror, and headed up her dirt road.

⚓   ⚓   ⚓

Maggie pulled into Stephenson's Funeral Home, shut off the truck, and sat there for a moment. Off to the west, the sky looked like someone had decided to put a tin roof over the bay, and Maggie heard a short succession of thunderclaps in the distance. Outside David's open window, a palmetto's dry, fan-like fronds rustled in the breeze, sounding like elderly ladies dressed in stiff old crinolines, hurrying away from inclement weather.

She took a deep breath and opened the truck door, cringing just a little at the familiar, metallic whine of rusty hinges. Then she slammed it shut and headed inside.

She was only in the red-carpeted lobby for a few seconds before she was greeted by a tall man with the build of someone who had played football long ago. His graying blond hair was molded into place, his gray pinstripe suit was perfectly pressed, and he wore what could only be described as a smile of perpetual sympathy.

"Good afternoon," he said smoothly as he walked into the reception area.

"Hello," Maggie said. "I'm Maggie Redmond. I'm here to, uh...pick up my ex-husband's remains."

"Yes, yes," he said softly, and held out a hand. Maggie took it. It was large, but plump and soft and overly warm. "I'm Benjamin Stephenson. We've met a few times over the years. Please accept my condolences on your husband's passing."

"Thank you," she said.

He spread an arm in the direction from which he had come. "Please come this way," he said, and Maggie followed him down a thickly carpeted hall to an expensively furnished, overly decorated office.

He indicated one of the maroon velvet armchairs that sat in front of a large cherry desk. "If you'll just have a seat, it won't take but a moment."

Maggie sat down, and Stephenson walked around the desk and sat down in the brown leather desk chair. Maggie read a small enamel plaque that promised eventual peace for those in grief while Stephenson opened a file drawer and rifled through a few manila folders.

"Yes, here we are," he said, pulling out one of the file folders. Maggie saw, as he laid it down, that it was labeled *Seward.* She thought about slapping the enamel plaque, but inspected a landscape on the wall instead.

Stephenson opened the folder and slipped out a white form with both yellow and pink copies attached in back. "I'll just need you to sign here, above your name. And also initial here. This is just a form accepting possession of your loved one's remains."

He handed Maggie a pen, and she glanced over the form, then signed and initialed as asked. He slid the form back to his side of the desk and slipped another out of the file, a stiff white card. "And here as well. And, although I know who you are, I will need to see your Driver's License. I apologize."

Maggie pulled her wallet out of her purse, and struggled to remove her license from the clear plastic window. As she did, she couldn't help noticing that the issue date was almost exactly five years ago. She had just gotten her divorce decree, and had gotten a new license with her old name. Now she wondered why that had seemed important.

She passed the license over to Stephenson, signed the card, and handed it to him, too. He gave her a warm smile, then copied her license number down on the first form, gently tore off the pink copy, and handed it to her.

"I'll be just a moment," he said as he stood. "Would you care for a bottled water or a cup of coffee?"

"No, thank you," Maggie said, twisting her hands in her lap.

He nodded and headed around his desk. "Please make yourself comfortable and I'll be right back with you."

After he'd gone, Maggie looked around the room. She supposed that the oil landscapes, simple floral arrangements, and vanilla oil candle were meant to comfort and calm. All they did was make her feel like she was exactly where she was, and had lost exactly what was gone.

She had just had the slightly panicked thought that, if she hurried back out the truck and left, she could somehow postpone reality, when Stephenson came back into the room, cradling a squat, dark blue jar in both hands.

Seeing it, seeing her husband being carried in the palms of another human being, was jarring, and she stood out of reflex, or maybe a desire to flee. She couldn't take her eyes off of the jar, as Stephenson came to stand in front of her.

"As per your and your husband's request, it's completely bio-degradable. It looks like pottery, but it's actually made of gelatin and sand. It will biodegrade in just a few weeks in soil, or about three days in water."

Maggie swallowed and nodded.

"The lid does remove easily, if you wish to scatter your loved one's ashes. You'll find, when you remove the lid, that there's a tab inside that will reveal a perforated cap for that purpose."

"Thank you," Maggie said, but barely.

"Is there anything else that I can do for you, Ms. Redmond?"

"No. Thank you."

"Very well." He extended his arms a bit, handed the jar out to her. "Again, you have my deepest sympathies, and the prayers of all of us at Stephenson's Funeral Home."

Maggie reached out and took the jar in both hands. It was impossible for her to comprehend, that David had been reduced to something that weighed fewer than five pounds, and took up less space than a gallon of milk.

"Thank you," she said for the third time, resting the jar against her stomach. Then she walked away from Stephenson's gentle smile without another word.

⚓ ⚓ ⚓

It took Maggie a few minutes to figure out what to do with the urn once she had gotten into the truck. She'd never even seen a cremation urn before, and it had all seemed so abstract when she and David had paid for the arrangements so long ago. She had thought that she would be elderly when she did see it, and that she would somehow know what to do with it, as though advanced age imparted secrets the young couldn't know.

Finally, she set it down in the passenger seat, wrapped the seat belt around it and buckled it in, then stuffed her purse up against it as well. Then she started the truck and drove away.

She pulled into the small grassy area that served as parking for Ten Hole Marina, a handful of boat slips near Battery Park that served as mooring for a handful of small houseboats and sailboats. She got out of the truck and shut the door, then opened it again and reached into the space behind the front seats, pulled out a beach towel, and draped it over the urn. Then she locked the truck and headed down the dock.

David's houseboat, a 38-foot white Burns Craft of 1970s vintage, was in the last slip. Maggie stepped aboard onto the small bow deck, where there was a pair of captain's chairs and a small plastic table. A coffee mug with a dried brown ring at the bottom sat on the table. Maggie ignored it and sifted through David's truck keys, found the one that opened the cabin door, and went inside.

The cabin was small and old, but it was neat and somewhat cozy. Maggie had entered into a cramped galley with just enough room for a booth. A few steps down to the left were the living area, with the stateroom and head beyond. Maggie stood there for a moment, gave herself just a few seconds to dwell on the fact that when David had last left, he had expected to come home. Then she stepped down into the living area.

The guitar that she'd bought for David was leaning up against an upholstered chair. Maggie went to it and picked it up gently by the neck. Then she walked over to a small, built in desk. There were two framed pictures on the shelf above the desk. One was of her and David, sitting on the deck in back of Boss Oyster, back when they'd still been married. The other was more recent, a shot of David and the kids from when they'd gone fishing last summer.

Maggie reached out to pick up the picture of her and David, and her hand stopped in mid-air. On the shelf beside it sat David's silver wedding band. She picked it up and stared at it, felt something pressing on her chest, then took a deep breath and shoved it into the front pocket of her jeans. Then she snatched up both of the pictures and hurried back outside.

TWENTY

M aggie was halfway home when Wyatt called.

"Hey," she answered.

"Hey, yourself. Where are you?"

"I'm on my way home. Where are you?"

"The office," he answered. "I have some news that I think you'll like hearing."

"What's going on?"

She heard some paper shuffling at the other end. "I've just finished going through David's bank statements for the last three years," Wyatt said. "For a little over two years, he'd been making weekly deposits into his savings account."

Maggie felt a part of her eager to get hopeful and she tried to talk it down. "Okay."

"No deposit was over a thousand dollars. Most of them were just a few hundred. As of his last deposit, dated June 19, he had $41,290.00. He purchased a cashier's check on June 27 for $39,500, made out to Gilbert Marine in Mobile, Al."

Maggie checked behind her for cars, then pulled over onto a small gravel turnaround. "David didn't steal anything," she said quietly.

"It doesn't look like it. Maybe it was for another reason, or maybe it was a mistake," Wyatt said. "But he saved up for the boat, just like he said."

Maggie put her head down on the steering wheel. "Thank you," she said.

"Are you okay?"

"Yes. I will be." She sat up and blew out a breath. "You have no food in your refrigerator."

There was silence on the other end for a moment, but Maggie thought she could hear Wyatt smiling when he spoke. "That's not true. I have two weeks' worth of leftovers in my refrigerator."

"I thought maybe you'd want to come over and let me cook you dinner."

"Well, I'd like to come over. I'll even eat. But you don't have to cook. I can bring something."

"From your fridge?"

"That's not nice."

"I'll cook. It relaxes me."

"Then I'll eat your real food," he said. "What time would you like me to present myself to you?"

"When are you leaving the office?"

"In about an hour. I do need to go home and shower, though."

Maggie looked at her ancient Timex. It was almost six. "Okay, well, just come over whenever you're ready."

They hung up, and Maggie looked over at the urn on the passenger seat, the pictures next to it, and the guitar on the floorboards.

He was still gone. But he hadn't done anything to make that happen. She felt like a piece of him had just been given back to her.

$$\updownarrow \quad \updownarrow \quad \updownarrow$$

When Maggie parked next to her Jeep in the gravel parking area, Coco had already barreled down the deck stairs and flung herself into the grass in front of the truck. Stoopid ran over her belly, flailed at Maggie with a half-hearted crow, then ran back across the yard, wings akimbo, looking like a failed experimental plane.

Maggie rubbed Coco's belly, then opened the passenger door and unbuckled the seat belt. Then she grabbed the guitar and the pictures, carefully picked up the urn, and carried everything inside, Coco at her heels.

She slid the urn gently onto the narrow table behind the couch, then set the guitar and pictures down. The thought occurred to her that David had finally come home, and she squashed it quick, lest it ruin her.

After grabbing a drink of water, she pulled some pork chops out of the fridge, seasoned them and set them aside, then went back into the living room. She leaned David's guitar up against the bookshelves he had built, and stood the pictures on top. Then she remembered David's wedding band, and pulled it out. She tucked it into her jewelry box in her room, a gift one day for Kyle.

She treated herself to a nice, long shower, put on some clean yoga pants and a tee shirt, and headed out to feed the girls for the night.

"No, Coco, not you," she said, as she opened the sliding door. "I don't need you tormenting the girls tonight."

Coco sat down, and Maggie pulled the door shut, ignoring the look of utter despair thrown her way.

She walked down to the chicken yard, relieved to feel rain in the air at last. It wasn't there yet, but it would be. She could taste it on her tongue. Chances were good that she and Wyatt would have to eat inside.

She got the cut-down milk jug from the shed, filled it with chicken feed, and walked over to the fence that surrounded the chicken yard. The dozen or so hens, a conglomeration of breeds, all came nattering over to the fence, exclaiming over their neglect and expressing their keen interest in having it rectified.

Stoopid came barreling in from everywhere, flapped a few times, and landed atop the fence next to Maggie.

"Dammit, Stoopid, I hate it when you—"

Something punched her in the front of her shoulder, and she lost her balance. She was halfway to the ground before she heard the shot.

She landed on her back. Oddly, she was still holding the feed jug, which landed upright and mostly full. Stunned, she glanced over at the fence, thinking for just a second that Stoopid was the one in danger. But he was gone and no one had come here to shoot her rooster.

Her brain finally started moving again, and she half sat up. Her shoulder screamed at her as she reached back for her weapon, but she realized that she'd never put her holster back on after her shower. Her .45 was still in her bedroom.

She was starting to get dizzy, and she could hear Coco going completely nuts inside the house. She looked up, and saw Coco jumping at the sliding glass door, saw the short, thin man in jeans and a Florida Marlins jersey walking across the yard to her.

She tried to focus on his face, but she knew she didn't know him anyway. She blinked a few times, virtually willed the fog away from her vision and her mind, as the man came to stop just a few feet away. He held a .22 down by his side.

"I'm tired of cleaning up Boudreaux's messes," he said quietly, and started to raise the gun.

Maggie swung the jug up toward his face and let it go, and she was up off of the ground before the seeds, pellets and a surprising amount of dust flew into his face. He was between her and the house, with nothing but a clear shot at her if she tried to get across the yard. She ran for the woods, just a few feet behind the chicken yard.

She could hear Coco losing her mind, her barking muffled and distant, but sounding so much more vicious than people gave her credit for. She could also hear the man swearing behind her, and another shot rang out. Maggie heard it whistle past to her right, as she veered to the left.

She knew she was at a serious disadvantage. She could no longer feel her left arm, and she was losing blood. But she knew these woods, all five, overgrown acres of them, like she knew the face of her firstborn child. If she could circle around to the left and come up on the far side of the house, she'd have some cover, and maybe enough time, to run up the deck stairs, get her damn gun, and blow this skinny trespasser out of his damn shoes.

She slowed her breathing, forcing herself to breathe only with her mouth closed so she wouldn't make too much noise, then soft-stepped around a clump of dead cypress trees that had been destroyed during a hurricane back in the 80s. She paused on the other side, listening. The crickets and cicadas were both at it, making it difficult to hear small noises, but she couldn't hear any footfalls or snapping twigs.

Although most of the woods offered good cover from overgrown thickets, she had ten feet of mostly open ground between her and the next good-sized bunch of trees, if she wanted to go the most direct route to the back of the house. She didn't, but her vision was blurring and she felt cold and nauseated. She needed to get into the house.

She had just stepped away from the old cypress, and was getting ready to run, when a hand reached out and grabbed the back of her shirt. She was pulled off balance before she could correct it, and when she turned and tried to raise her arm to fight back, her arm never materialized.

She raised a leg instead, and managed to kick at his hand. While she did manage to make him lose his grip on his gun, she didn't kick it very far. Her kick was too weak and his arm too high for her wonky balance. She suddenly realized that Coco's barking had gotten much louder and clearer, and was actually moving closer, and she had just enough time to wonder how Coco had gotten out, and to worry for her safety, before a fist snapped out and dropped her to the ground.

She fell back hard against the cypress, a wood as hard as stone, and felt her head smash against it as she did. Bright lights exploded inside her skull, and as she fell, she heard a crunching in the leaves, Coco's insane growl, and the gunshot.

TWENTY-ONE

aggie blinked a few times, her head coming apart each time, then felt Coco's tongue on her face. She reached up with her good arm, eyes unfocused, and grabbed Coco's collar. "Coco, go!" she said, and shoved her away. The tongue was back instantly, and Maggie heard heavy footsteps on the ground, heard them stop just behind her head.

He crouched down and his face entered her line of vision. His eyebrows were knitted together underneath his ball cap. "The security code is four-zero-nine-eight," Wyatt said tiredly. "Next time, use it."

He reached over and put his hand on her back, gently rolled her halfway toward him. He pulled the collar of her tee shirt down and looked at the back of her shoulder. "Clean through."

He put one hand on her waist and the other under her good arm, and pulled her up to a sitting position. She saw the skinny man a few feet away, face down in the dirt.

"Is that Fain?" she asked weakly.

"No. Just some dead guy." He put his face in her face, forcing her to look at him. "Maybe he was irritated with you, too," he said, but Maggie saw his eyes moisten.

"If I help you, can you stand up?" he asked.

Maggie gave him something that was half shrug and half head shake. "Yeah," she said.

Wyatt sighed and helped her up. Coco licked at Maggie's hand, which hung limp and forgotten at her side.

"Well, let's get you up to the house and call it in." He started walking, leaning her against his side. Coco jingled behind them. "Then you can start dinner."

⚓ ⚓ ⚓

Early the next morning, Boudreaux was sitting across from Miss Evangeline at the kitchen table. The local paper was a weekly, and not published on Sunday, so he had the Tallahassee paper in its plastic bag beside his placemat.

He watched Miss Evangeline reorganize her flatware into some microscopically different configuration that was somehow better than the original, as he stirred his second cup of coffee. The smell of bacon assaulted him from the kitchen island, where Amelia stood over her cast iron skillet, spatula in the air.

Boudreaux was tired, and he was tired of thinking. He needed things to proceed in an orderly fashion, and the things didn't seem to want to do that. People. People interfered with the rightful order of things.

Miss Evangeline looked up at him, the early sunlight reflecting off of her thick lenses and making her look like she had flashlights for eyes. She glanced at the paper beside him, then looked him somewhere in the vicinity of his eyes.

"I need you go through them coupon, find me one to get my hair cut," she said

Boudreaux sighed. "Why? You only have seven."

She raised her chin just a little, presumably to get a better look at him. Then she made that irritated little clicking sound she made. "I see your sass got up wit' you this mornin'," she said. "I pass you a slap you don't forget."

She looked over at Amelia. "'melia, bring me a flippy-turny."

Amelia sighed as she flipped the bacon over in the pan. "I don't have time for y'all nonsense. You want a spatula, you come get it."

Boudreaux was about to say something when he heard the clicking of heels behind him, and saw Miss Evangeline sit up straighter.

"Amelia, is my tea ready?" he head Lily ask.

"Yes, ma'am, it is."

Lily tapped over to the island, her fuchsia Diane von Somebody dress swishing with each step, and picked up a cup and saucer. She took the tea bag out of the cup and dropped it onto the counter, then turned to face Boudreaux.

"Are you coming to Mass?"

"Yes," he said, picking up his coffee.

"Good," Lily said, then gave him a tight smile. "You can pray for your little girlfriend."

Boudreaux's cup stopped just shy of his mouth. "What girlfriend?"

"Maggie Redmond, sweetheart. It was just on the radio."

"What was on the radio?' he asked, a light, fluttering sensation starting in his chest.

"She was shot," Lily said, the corners of her mouth turned up just a bit. "They released her from the hospital late last night."

"Released her."

"Yes, apparently she'll live." She started tapping back across the kitchen. "I guess she has enemies. Either that or someone just got tired of her."

She left the room, and Boudreaux set down his cup very carefully, stared into it.

"I tol' you not to marry that fruit bat lookin' woman," Miss Evangeline said. "Her and 'em no good boys a hers. Nothin' but thirty-five years of misery."

"If it's any consolation, I think her mouth is becoming too tight for her to speak properly," Boudreaux said distractedly.

"Juju."

"And I thank you for it."

$$\text{⚓ ⚓ ⚓}$$

Maggie stood in the driveway of her parents' home, cell phone in hand, and watched her mother's car pull in. Coco sat beside her, doing one of her sit-down wiggles. She obviously wanted to run to the car, but she hadn't left Maggie's side since she'd come back from the ER.

She waited, as her children jumped out of each back door.

"Mom!" Kyle yelled, and ran up to hug her, then stopped and leaned in gently, avoiding the sling holding her right arm.

Maggie hugged him with one arm, buried her nose in his hair, and breathed deeply of her child. Then she smiled at Sky, who had come to stand beside them.

Sky wrapped an arm around her mother and tucked her face into her good shoulder. "We were so scared," she said quietly.

"It's all okay," Maggie said, and kissed the side of her head. "We're okay."

Gray came up, took Maggie's head in his hands, and bent it forward so he could kiss her forehead. "It's good to see you, Sunshine." When he let her go, he was blinking away tears.

"It's good to see you guys," Maggie said. She accepted a hug from her mother, who didn't bother blinking away anything. "It's just really good to see you."

"Where's Wyatt?" Georgia asked. "I thought he was taking care of you."

"He'll be back," Maggie said. "He had to go to work."

They started walking toward the front door. Gray put a hand on her good shoulder, like it wasn't okay yet to break contact.

"Poor Wyatt," Georgia said. "He was just a mess when he called us last night."

"Please, Mom," Maggie said. "Wyatt's never a mess."

Gray gently padded her shoulder. "Honey, sometimes you're just so smart. And other times, you have nothing going on up there at all."

⚓ ⚓ ⚓

Maggie spent the rest of the day resting, being plied with collard greens and chicken soup, and hanging onto her kids. It occurred to her several times during the day, as it had several times in the emergency room, that it wasn't fair for her kids to come so close to losing both parents, and in such a short span of time. For the first time, she began to question whether she should continue in her line of work.

Wyatt joined them for dinner that night, and then the kids, both of them exhausted, turned in early. The adults had a glass of wine, and talked about the events of the last several days. They talked about adjustments, and peace and a certainty of healing. It was, eventually, more than Maggie had the energy to bear, and she asked Wyatt to come get some air with her.

They crossed the long, narrow back yard, went through the gate in the chain link fence, and sat down on the end of Gray's dock. There was an unseasonably pleasant breeze, and the palms all sounded content as they rustled their fronds, like they were stretching after a too hot afternoon.

Maggie and Wyatt sat for a few minutes without speaking, watching as the lights of a few shrimp boats crossed the dark bay.

"So who was this guy Harper?" Maggie asked of the skinny dead man.

"I don't know that much," Wyatt answered. "He did fourteen years at Stark for second-degree murder. Lived in Eastpoint. Has two arrests for beating his wife, charges dropped. Has one outstanding charge of aggravated assault, was supposed to go to trial next month."

"How did he even make bail?"

"Paid it. $20,000."

Maggie looked over at Wyatt. "Any connection to Fain?"

"Not that I know of. Yet."

Maggie hadn't told Wyatt what the skinny man had said about cleaning up Boudreaux's messes. She wasn't even sure yet why. She knew that withholding things from Wyatt, as she had been doing, was no way to start a relationship. But Boudreaux was messy and convoluted, and she wanted some time to work it out in her mind, and then work out how to be honest.

She looked back out to the bay for a few minutes. "Will you come with us tomorrow night?" she finally asked.

It took Wyatt a moment to answer. "If you want me to."

"You don't have to if you don't want to."

"I do," he said.

TWENTY-TWO

aggie walked down to the end of the dock behind Sea-Fair, and stopped at the beautiful wooden 1947 Chris Craft that Boudreaux had restored to perfection. Boudreaux had his back to Maggie, was polishing the trim on the helm.

There was a moderate wind, and the promise of rain, but it would be light if it came. It was close to sunset, and the air had cooled enough to be bearable.

"Hello, Mr. Boudreaux," Maggie said.

Boudreaux turned around, and he looked a little taken aback, just for a moment. Whether it was from seeing her splinted and bandaged, or seeing her alive at all, she didn't know.

"Hello, Maggie," he said quietly.

They looked at each other a moment, Maggie with her good hand resting atop her sling, Boudreaux with his rag in his hands.

"I heard what happened. Are you all right?"

"Yes, thank you," Maggie said. The breeze whipped her long hair into her face. She pulled it back with her good hand, held it there. I was just down the docks and saw you over here."

She shook her hair out of her face and took a breath.

"Mr. Boudreaux, do you remember that night at Boss Oyster? The night that Grace Carpenter jumped from the bridge?"

He seemed a little surprised by the question, as though he expected a different one entirely. "Yes."

"You shared your scotch with me. You were very kind," she said.

"You needed kindness."

Maggie nodded slightly. "It was a few days after your nephew's funeral." It had also been a couple of days after Wilmette had visited the Sea-Fair office.

"Yes."

"You said you were going night fishing. With a friend," she said. "How was it?"

Boudreaux looked down at the rag in his hands, folded it, and set it down. "I wasn't going out to fish," he said. "I was with a woman friend, Maggie."

"Ah," Maggie said, nodding.

"Why do you ask?"

"It's not important," she said. "Have a good night."

Boudreaux looked at her with those incredible blue eyes, the wind blowing his thick hair over his brow. He ignored it. "Good night, Maggie."

Maggie turned and started back up the dock, then stopped after a few steps and turned around. He was still watching her.

"Did you try to hurt me, Mr. Boudreaux?" she asked quietly.

Boudreaux shook his head slowly. "No, Maggie. I didn't."

Maggie looked at hm for a moment. He didn't look away. Then she nodded again and walked back the way she'd come.

She crossed the back of the Sea-Fair parking lot, and headed down to the docks belonging to Scipio, just a few hundred feet away. Axel's trawler was warming up, and Maggie's parents, Sky, and Kyle were already aboard.

Wyatt pulled up as Maggie reached the slip, and she waited for him to reach her.

"You doing okay?" he asked her.

"Yeah," she said. "Go ahead, I'll get the stern line."

Wyatt stepped aboard, and Maggie grabbed the line and jumped on. The kids were sitting on one of the shrimp boxes, the dark blue urn between them. Gray and Georgia stood at the port rail.

Maggie stowed the line, then she and Wyatt sat down on the box across from the kids, and Axel nodded at Maggie and pulled away from the dock.

It took them a good thirty minutes to get out to David's favorite hole, not too far past St. George Island. By the time they got to it, it was nearly dark. The breeze had calmed a bit with the setting of the sun, and there was just a touch of purple and orange left to the sky at the horizon line.

Axel cut the engine and dropped the sea anchor, then walked over to where Maggie and Wyatt had gone to stand at the stern rail. "This is it, Maggie," he said. It was the first time she'd seen him without a cigarette since they were about sixteen.

Maggie nodded and looked at the kids. They stood up, and were joined by their grandparents. Sky carried the urn in her arms, and handed it to Maggie, then took her cell phone back from Kyle.

Maggie looked at Sky, and Sky looked at the urn, then looked at her phone. She tapped it, and her playlist lit up.

She tapped again, and "Waterbound" by Dirk Powell began to play. David's favorite song, and the one Maggie had requested most from him.

"Sky?" Maggie spoke softly.

Sky looked at the urn again. "I love you, Daddy."

Maggie looked at Kyle. "Bye, Daddy," he said.

Maggie looked at Georgia, but Georgia had her eyes closed, her hand over her mouth.

"We love you, son," Gray said quietly.

Maggie turned around and stepped up to the rail, then remembered she only had one hand. She turned to ask Wyatt if he could open it, but he was already there. While she held the urn, he removed the lid, and then pulled the small tab inside.

"Thank you," Maggie said.

Then she tilted the urn over the side, almost parallel to the water, and watched a small stream of nearly-white powder begin to flow, most of it blowing east before hitting the surface of the water.

She held the urn over the water until the ashes stopped coming, then dropped the urn into the water, where it bobbed on a gentle wave. Wyatt started to back away, but Maggie reached out and took his hand in her one good one, then watched as the urn began to sink.

"I love you, David," Maggie whispered. "Break the nets."

⚓ ⚓ ⚓

THE END

Read on for a sneak peek at *What Washes Up,* the third book in the Forgotten Coast Suspense series.

www.dawnleemckenna.com

GET UNFORGOTTEN

To get UnForgotten, and be the first to hear about new releases, special pricing for friends of the series and fun news about the books and Apalach, please subscribe to the newsletter.

I'd like to extend a special thank you to so many of you who pre-ordered your copy of Riptide.

You let me know after reading *Low Tide* that you wanted to keep reading this series almost as much as I want to keep writing it. I was overwhelmed by the number of pre-orders, and it meant a great deal to me that you wanted to spend more time with these characters. It's because of you that I knew that Maggie, Wyatt and Boudreaux had an audience.

As always, your honest review would be deeply appreciated. If you could take a moment to share your experience with *Riptide,* I would be thrilled.

Also, feel free to drop me a line anytime, at

dawnmckenna63@gmail.com

I love hearing from readers.

CHAPTER ONE

t was a windy night out on the bay, very windy for a late-July night without any tropical storms in the area.

Maggie Redmond's long, dark brown hair kept trying to fly out of its clip, and she struggled to get it all tucked and out of her way one-handed. Her right arm, the one she really had a close relationship with, was still in a sling, after she'd been shot by some low-life on her own property.

She gave up on the clip and grabbed onto the portside rail, then looked up at Wyatt Hamilton, who was towering over her, holding binoculars to his face as he looked out to the bay.

She, Wyatt, and Dwight, one of the deputies who worked with them at the Sheriff's office, had taken her Dad's fishing boat out past St. George Island to do a little sunset fishing. Wyatt had just been reeling in a nice-sized redfish when they got the call.

It probably wasn't especially appropriate for them to respond, given that Dwight had had a few beers, Maggie was on leave and one-armed, and Wyatt didn't look especially Sheriff-y in his cargo shorts and red Hawaiian shirt. However, they were already halfway to the location, and would beat the Coast Guard by at least five minutes.

"Can you make anything out yet?" she yelled over the Chris Craft's engine.

"Not really," Wyatt barked. "It's too dark. But they're right, it is on fire."

Michael Vinton and Richard Farrell, two shrimpers that Maggie knew only passingly, had come upon it as they were headed out for the night's work. They'd called the Coast Guard and the Sheriff's Office, and someone at the office had called Wyatt.

Dwight was with them, so it wasn't technically their third date, but Wyatt was a little put out, nonetheless.

"Let me look," Maggie yelled up at him. She was short to begin with, but being one-armed besides made her feel even smaller next to Wyatt, who, at six-four, was more than a foot taller than she was.

"No," Wyatt said. "You have one hand and Dwight's hitting every damn wave like he was getting points for it. You'll drop my binoculars."

"No, I won't. Let me look."

"I said 'no,'" Wyatt told her.

He took the binoculars down, looked at her, and gave her an eyebrow waggle. "My mom got me these."

Maggie shook her head and sat down on one of the bench seats. She and Wyatt had worked together at the Sheriff's Office for six years, had become friends who flirted over the last two, and had only started seeing each other over the last several weeks. It was, of course, forbidden by the department, so they'd been keeping it quiet. This was fairly easy thus far, as most people thought they acted like an old married couple anyway.

The banter was part of their friendship and they both counted on it to keep things sane. But their feelings ran deeper, and belied their sarcastic and often teasing mode of communication. Wyatt had lost his wife to cancer shortly before moving to Apalachicola, and Maggie's friendship had helped him heal. Maggie had lost her ex-husband, who was also her best friend, just a few short weeks ago. Wyatt was helping her heal, too. Nonetheless, she thought he was a jerk.

She watched the orange glow in the middle of the bay as it grew larger, and could make out Michael and Richard in the lights of their trawler, anchored just yards away. They were standing at the stern rail, watching the small fire.

A few minutes later, Dwight cut the engine, and they coasted up to about ten yards from the flames. The shrimp boat's engine was silent as well, and suddenly the only sounds Maggie heard were the hiss and pop of the flames and the lapping of the wake as it slapped at the sides of the boat.

"What the hell?" Wyatt asked, as he and Maggie walked to the starboard rail and looked at what they'd come for.

It was a small oyster skiff, a wooden one, but she didn't recognize it. The paint had been scratched or blasted off of the stern, leaving no name to identify her, at least, not straightaway. But the lack of a name, and even the fact that it was on fire, weren't the details that stood out the most. The man hanging from the front of the cabin, and currently offering his lower body to the flames, was a little more interesting.

"Good grief," Maggie said. "What the hell is this?"

"Well, we don't get too many Viking funerals around here," Wyatt said. "So I don't think it's that."

He grabbed one of the long metal fish hooks from its holder and poked at the burning skiff to keep them from bumping. Then he bent over sideways, to look up at the face.

Meanwhile, Dwight began making motions like a cat with a hair ball, and Wyatt heard him coughing into his hand.

"Ya all right, Dwight?" Wyatt asked.

"Yeah. Yeah, but, uh, the smell. I'm a vegetarian."

"Well, don't worry. I wasn't going to invite you to try a bite."

Dwight took two steps to the port side and threw his beer up over the rail.

"Sorry," Wyatt said.

Maggie stood at the starboard rail beside Wyatt and sniffed. Aside from the rather horrid odor of burning flesh, she could pick up no kerosene, diesel or other fuel that might have been used as an accelerant. That would help explain why it was burning so slowly.

"Well, this night's just getting better and better," Wyatt said, standing up.

"What?"

"That's Rupert Fain."

"What?"

Rupert Fain was the drug dealer that was suspected of being behind the blowing up of her ex-husband on his shrimp boat at the town's 3rd of July celebration. They'd been looking for him since.

"It's Fain. I memorized his damn mug shot."

"He's from Gainesville. What's he doing out here?"

"Pondering the existence of karma, I imagine."

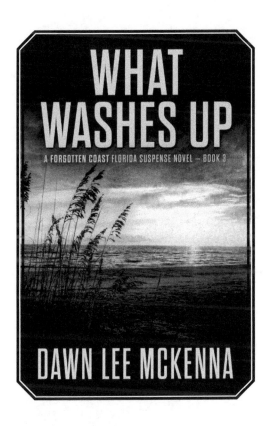

What Washes Up will be released on or before July 16th.

You can preorder your copy at:

amazon.com/Dawn-Lee-McKenna/e/B00RC14PPG

CPSIA information can be obtained
at www.ICGtesting.com
Printed in the USA
LVHW050304270419
615789LV00005B/25/P